TUBAR

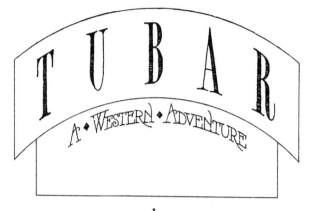

TUBAR

A · WESTERN · ADVENTURE

by

John Tilley

SUNSTONE PRESS

FIRST EDITION   Printed in the United States of America

Library of Congress Cataloging in Publication Data
Tilley, John, 1929-
        Tubar / by John Tilley. — 1st ed.
              p.   cm.
          ISBN 0-86534-181-8 : $12.95
          I. Title.
PS3570 . I3636T8   1992
813' .54—dc20   92-10355
                                       CIP

Published by SUNSTONE PRESS
              Post Office Box 2321
              Santa Fe, NM 87504-2321 / USA

This novel is dedicated to my Riding Partners.

A Tilley Fiction Western

New Mexico Registered Brand

LOSING A PARTNER

The street was suddenly quiet. And Red looked up when Bill spoke to him. The older man was almost doubled over. His left hand was covering a big hole in his chest. Blood was spurting between his fingers.

"BILL . . . NO!" Red yelled, as Bill stepped back in an attempt to keep his balance. Red dragged himself forward, trying to keep up. Then Bill was on his back.

"O GOD! You can't die on me!"

Bill touched Red's face. And his fingers came away wet. "Will you tell Starlet that I've always loved her?"

Red was crying. "I'll tell her!"

"And tell her she can have my . . . my . . ."

"YOU BASTARDS!" Red screamed, and brought his Colt up. Only to have it taken away from him.

One

"YOUNG MAN! You are banished forever from Bramsley!"

Kicked out of the Bramsley School for Boys, and disgraced, Tubar Lane ran his eyes over the high gray walls of the school's buildings. They were richly covered by a heavy growth of climbing vines. With an abundance of white flowers reflecting the light from a full-moon. The scene around him was one of peace and tranquility. But there was no peace in Tubar. Nor tranquility.

He turned his six-foot two hundred twenty pound frame and took in the rest of Chapel Hill. Where Bramsley School was located. Where he was being tutored in advanced reading and figures. And was on the boxing and wrestling teams. Tubar shook his mop of wavy blood-red hair. And felt a gush of tears flood his eyes. He brushed them away with a stubby finger attached to a big right hand. Tubar was glad that it was late at night. That no one was around to see a seventeen year old man on the verge of crying. For he felt himself a man.

Tubar thought of his Father. Stern, unbending and religious. And Tubar would've finished school in two more weeks. Now he could not return home. To Wheeling, to a Father who too often had informed his son that he was like his worthless Mother. Now the son, like the woman who gave Raymond Lane his only child, was running too. Tubar's Father had never remarried.

The young man picked up a large valise which contained everything he now possessed. And with hammering head, a queasy stomach, a severely sore body, he walked to the middle of the street. Then started the long three-mile trek to the Baltimore & Ohio railroad yard. This was in Baltimore, Maryland. The year 1872, a Tuesday, and the May fourteenth summer night was warm.

Tubar's disgraceful exit from the school had foiled his Father's plans to have him work as a bookkeeper in the family's freighting business. And Tubar let his thoughts go back in time. To about thirty hours ago.

A tavern located at the foot of Chapel Hill was a student hang-out. The owner of The Boars Head allowed them to use a small room in the back. One with a private door through which they could enter and leave unseen. Even Chancellor McElroy was unaware of the room. And he frequented the tavern too.

Tubar and several companions had slipped out of their dormitories and gone to the tavern. One of the students was Brad Wallace. And he and Brad were competing for the attention of the same beautiful girl. Brad's family owned a large cattle stockyard in Chicago . . . and Tubar's a freighting company. This made the competition about even.

And after three draughts of ale, Brad suggested they go to The Sailor's Cove. Another tavern located on the wharf. Thinking back on this had Tubar frowning. He'd wondered about the carriage they found conveniently waiting outside The Boars Head.

The arrival of the students inside The Sailor's Cove almost silenced the place. Sea faring men of every age and nationality watched them approach the bar. This was the roughest tavern on the wharf . . . maybe in the whole of Baltimore. . .where a man could get killed or shanghaied onto an out-going ship. Tubar was mulling on this when he reached for the ale a bartender set in front of him. It was the last thing he remembered. Until waking up in bed with one of the tavern whores. This was several hours later. . . in the middle of the following afternoon.

And while Tubar was trying to wash the cheap smell of the sleeping woman off him . . . two Constables entered the room. They delivered him to Chancellor McElroy. Who was waiting outside the tavern.

The carriage ride back to the school was made longer by the tongue-lashing Tubar was receiving. But the younger man wasn't paying a lot of heed to the Chancellor's harsh words. His mind was on Brad Wallace . . . and trying to remember what a certain bartender looked like. The man that served him an ale with a mickey finn in it.

Tubar was ordered to stay in his dormitory until the Chancellor sent for him on the following Wednesday. But instead, he looked for Brad. Who was absent from his quarters . . . and no one knew his whereabouts. Or would tell. Tubar left the school's grounds, while thinking the low-life bastard could be found later.

He began walking down Chapel Hill . . . in the direction of The Sailor's Cove. And came to an ice-wagon that was ready to pull away from The Boars Head.

"I'm headed for The Sailor's Cove!" Tubar said to the deliveryman. "Can I work my way as far as you're going?"

The man grinned, while taking stock of the stout-looking lad. "You sure as hell can! I can use some strong help! And my last stop is at the Cove!"

* * * *

Tubar used a strong pair of ice-tongs to pull the large block of ice onto his left shoulder. Then followed the delivery-man into The Sailor's Cove. He carried the heavy load to the back of the building and deposited it in a cold . . . thick-walled storage room. Then returned to the barroom.

"Damn!" He exclaimed to the familiar face behind the bar, "There's blood all over the floor!"

"The hell there is! I'll kill that damn swamper!" And the bartender leaned over the structure to have a look.

Tubar pulled the screaming man over the bar like he was a block of ice. One sharp point of the tongs was in the bartender's chest . . . the other in his back. Tubar kept the tongs in place with his right hand, and smashed a big left fist into the man's mouth. Lips split, blood flowed, and three upper front teeth disappeared.

"WHO PAID YOU TO FIX MY DRINK!" Tubar yelled, and the barroom was suddenly quiet.

"GET HIM OFF! HE'S KILLING ME!"

"Tell me . . . or I will kill you!"

"It was Brad Wallace! One of your buddies! He was playing a joke on you!" And the bartender screamed again. "HELP ME SOME-BODY!"

Tubar punched the man in the mouth again. He removed the tongs. Then met the customers coming at him with the heavy metal tongs and his left fist. But the wave of older men, and the punches and kicks they were meting-out, were too much for the lad. He was thrown bodily out of the tavern. And delivered to Chancelor McElroy again. Bruised, sore, and almost sick from a bad hangover. The Chancellor didn't return him to the dormitory this time. But bounced him out of school.

"And good ole Master Schieman!" Tubar said out loud, as he drew closer to the railroad yard. "He tried to talk McElroy out of expelling me!"

When this didn't work, Master Schieman left the Chancellor's office. To return and push a small leather pouch deep into Tubar's left-front trouser pocket. He placed a package in the valise. Then hugged the younger man. "You have a good future ahead of you, son! Go find it!"

Tubar thought of his words. Then let his mind picture Elsa Stewart. Her nice athletic legs, and long black hair which she wore in a bun at the back of her head. The girl he had hoped to marry one day. He was already hurting too much . . . to suffer greatly over her loss to Brad Wallace.

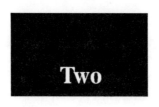

Two

A new day, Wednesday, May the fifteenth, 1872, was dawning when Tubar arrived at the west end of the yard. He remained on the side of a brush and tree covered hill. To run his eyes over the many lines of railroad tracks below him. Then took special note of the engines being readied. Which were evidenced by columns of heavy smoke coming from the stacks. And the engines pointing in a western direction.

A hungry Tubar Lane was slowly recovering from the mickey finn he'd drank hours earlier. He stayed on the hillside, out of sight, and sat on the ground. He removed the pouch from his pocket. Opened it and emptied the contents onto the palm of his left hand. Then stared at several pieces of gold money. Double-Eagles . . . all eighteen of them, and he was in possession of three hundred sixty dollars, His heart warmed as he thought of Master Schieman again. His good friend, and the one who was teaching him his figures.

Then Tubar reached into the bag. Took the package out and opened it. There was a large piece of cheese, bread, and a wrapped long-barrelled revolver. He picked the pistol up and saw that it was a forty caliber five-shot single action Colt. The weapon was loaded in four chambers. With the empty chamber under the hammer.

"That damn thing is kind of old!" A deep voice said from Tubar's left. "But it'll do the job!"

Tubar pointed the barrel at the sound. With his finger on the trigger. "Come out here where I can see you!" A much smaller man than he expected came into view. Because of the deep voice.

"Now don't get carried away, son! I'm keeping both hands on this bedroll! Where you can see them!" The stranger measured the younger man. And took stock of his clothing, which at one time was clean and ironed, He ran his eyes over the wavy red hair, an abundance of freckles, and large hairy arms. Then stopped on a discolored face. Both eyes were puffy and black, "You've been in one hell of a mean fight! Was it man or panther?"

The words made Tubar grin, more than the way they sounded. But the Colt didn't waver. "It was man! Where are you from?"

An amused look came into the little man's eyes. "I hail from out west! And in some places it isn't healthy to ask an hombre where he's from!" Then he continued. "I'm no threat to you. . . or to all that dinero you're carrying!"

Tubar started his inspection at the man's boots. Then looked at his trousers. Tubar let his eyes linger on a spot around the man's waist and down his right trouser leg. The large area wasn't as faded as the rest of his well-worn trousers. The inspection was complete when Tubar took stock of the faded shirt, his blue eyes, graying hair, and large hat, "Are you armed?"

"Yep! And point that .40 in another direction. . .or use it!" The blue eyes watched the long barrel being lowered to the ground. "My name's Bill Compton! I've been west of the Mississippi working as a cowhand. And came back looking for a girl I used to know. But she's long gone!"

Tubar nodded his head. While making a decision. Then returned the Colt to the valise. And offered his right hand in friendship. "I'm Tubar Lane. . .and was just kicked out of school!"

Bill Compton shook the hand. "You talk like a school boy! But I won't hold that against you! Now tell me where you're going!"

Tubar shrugged his shoulders. "I don't know! A bartender slipped me a mickey finn, and that's when my troubles started!"

He told Bill what had happened during the past several hours. "I can't go home! My Father is a pillar of the community!"

"Are you on good terms with your Pa?"

"No. . . he's so bad at times that my Mother ran-off when I was two years old!" And the younger man continued, while pointing at the trains. "I'm going west on one of those!"

"Have you ridden the rails before?"

"No sir!"

"Well . . . you've got more schooling in front of you! And don't start-out by calling me. . . sir!"

Tubar laughed. "Are you going to teach me the ropes?"

"Yep! And I don't usually saddle myself with a maverick! But you show some promise!"

"What's a maverick?"

"A calf that's lost from its Ma." Bill watched Tubar grin, and continued. "Can you handle that Colt pistol?"

"I usually hit what I aim at."

"I'll teach you another way to shoot one! But keep that Colt handy until then! We'll be seeing some mean sons of bitches along the track!"

"Where'd you leave your mount?"

"In St. Louis!" And Bill pointed at the yard. "See that closest engine! The one easing this way! It was made by the Baldwin Locomotive Works right after the big fight between the States! They call it a Mogul, and it's pulling a freight train straight to Grafton, and on to St. Louis! We'll be on it!"

"Do we board it here?"

Bill laughed at his new companion. "No, Tubar! And we don't hop it here either! The Bulls' would just kick us off! We'll make our move down the track from here! Come on! You can eat while we walk!"

Tubar followed his friend away from the railroad yard. And was occupied with a small piece of the bread and cheese.

Bill watched Tubar put the rest back in the bag. Then nodded his head with approval. "Do you have any water?"

"Nope! That's the one thing I didn't think of!"

"I have a full canteen! We'll get by until you can buy one!"

Bill stopped talking when they came to a trestle crossing a small creek. He led the way until they were under the bridge. Then seated himself on the ground, and reached inside the bed-roll. The hand came out holding a canteen. He drank his fill and handed it to Tubar. "Drink what you can of this! And fill it with fresh water! We'll eat and drink when we can . . . and won't when we can't!"

Tubar drank what he could, and refilled the container at the creek. He returned and pointed at the valise. "You're welcome to share the food I have!" Then Tubar cocked his head to one side. And listened to a strange sound.

"That's the rails' singing!" Bill said, and continued, "Our ride is on the way! I'll pick the car . . . and you be certain to hop the rear end of it!"

He waited until the pulling engine had labored to the far side of the trestle and was out of sight. Then scrambled up the bank with Tubar hot on his heels°

Bill ran in the direction they had come from. And stopped to watch the passing boxcars. He timed his walk to one, and seemingly without effort, grabbed the side-ladder and was lifted off the ground.

The younger man watched this maneuver out of the corner of his right eye. Then the end of the car was in front of him. He also grabbed the ladder, and was jerked off the ground. It felt as if his arms were being ripped from his body . . . and only brute strong hands saved him from the trailing car's wheels and certain death.

Tubar pulled himself onto the ladder, and climbed to the top of the boxcar. He was facing a laughing Bill Compton. "That looked easy when you did it!"

"My way takes a lot of practice! You run alongside the car, and hop-on when the ladder gets to you!" Bill explained. "Come on up! We can lie down on the top of this thing while its away from towns! We don't have boards for riding the rods!"

"What happens when we get to a town?"

"Nothing until we arrive at Grafton! There's a big yard in that place . . . and a tough Railroad Bull! We'll land in jail if he catches us!"

Tubar seated himself beside Bill. They were at the middle of the car. The younger man thought of what he'd said. "Are you broke?"

"Almost! I can buy a little food on the way . . . and pay for the keep on my horse. Or I'll lose him!"

"I have money!" Tubar continued. "We'll get off on this side of Grafton, and ride a rail-coach to St. Louis! I don't want to start my new life in a damn jail!"

* * * *

They left the railroad's right-of-way about two miles out of Grafton, West Virginia. A part of Virginia that had supported the Union. And Bill was keeping his eyes on a very stiff companion. The long hours of sitting and lying on the moving boxcar had taken their toll.

"How bad off are you?"

"I'm one big hurt!" Tubar answered, from behind a pale face and tight lips.

"Did they break any ribs?"

Tubar shook his head. "I hurt about the same all over! It'll ease-up after I've walked a bit!"

"What started the ruckus, son?"

"Part of it was over a girl another student and I liked! His name is Brad Wallace . . . from Chicago! The rest is because I whipped him in a boxing meet!"

"Is this Brad part of the Stockyard Wallaces?" Bill watched Tubar nod his head this time. As the younger man struggled along the road they were on. "I know some of the family! Most of the man are ornery bastards!"

And Bill continued. While changing the subject. "How old were you when your Ma cut-out?"

"I was two! And all I can remember about her. . . is that she was so much taller than me!"

Bill laughed. "She must have looked as high as a mountain! Was she redheaded too?"

"My Father said her hair was the same deep red as mine! And he hasn't had any use for a redheaded person since Mother disappeared!"

"Hell, Tubar! Why didn't she take you along?"

"I don't know!" He answered, as they entered the town. "It's the part that hurts!"

Bill spotted a bathhouse. Where they could clean-up for twenty-five cents. And he headed for it. Then asked another question. "What was her name?"

"Starlet! The name and the red hair is all I know about my Mother!"

A less hurting Tubar Lane would've seen Bill's head turn quickly, so he could stare at him. And there was a curious look in the older man's eyes. But Bill stopped asking questions, and led the way into the bathhouse. Where he gave the operator two twenty-five cent shin plasters.

"My young amigo here," Bill said to him, "needs a tub of hot water! He was in a bad fight!"

The man grinned. While looking at Tubar's face. "I've been in one or two mean brawls! Follow me!"

They trailed the operator through another doorway leading to a back room. Then watched him leave. It was a large room, and contained twelve big wooden tubs.

Bill stripped to the skin. Stepped into a tub of warm water, and then looked at Tubar. The boy was naked as a jaybird too. And he looked like a spotted horse. His freckles were many. . . and a lot of them were covered by huge, dark blue and purple bruises.

"MY GOD! What did they beat you with?"

Tubar grinned, while surveying his chest and ribs. "Fists and feet! I was swinging a big pair of ice-tongs at them! That's what I used to drag the bartender to my side of the bar!"

Bill shook his head, While wishing he'd seen the fight, And watched the operator return with a large bucket of steaming water.

"You pour it!" The man said to Tubar. And shuddered while looking him over. "That way I won't be blamed if the water is too hot!"

And Bill waited until Tubar had heated the water already in the tub to a suitable temperature. Then continued. "How come the bastards didn't kill you?"

Tubar settled himself in the water before answering. "They knew I was a Bramsley student. That must have kept me alive!"

* * * *

The slow freight-train ride from Baltimore to Grafton had taken from Thursday morning . . . to the middle of Friday morning.

Bill and Tubar left the bathhouse clean and in a change of clothing. Bill in his last presentable outfit. And Tubar in his. The younger man now had a lighter valise too. Weighing less . . . because Bill said they would buy new outfits in St. Louis. Designed to make Tubar look less the greenhorn. Tubar promptly gave most of his spare clothes to the man who supplied the hot water. A bath that had removed a lot of stiffness and soreness.

And unlike the warm sunny world they left upon entering the establishment . . . a warm rainy world awaited them. Tubar whistled down a carriage, and watched the driver swing the two-horse team around. Then pull-up beside them.

"Take us to the train depot! Then we want something to eat!"

"There's an eating house at the depot. The ride will cost you fifty cents!"

They climbed into the carriage. After Bill had surrendered a four-bit shin plaster. And the ride to the depot took them all of five minutes.

Bill waited until they were out of the carriage and in the depot before speaking. "Well . . . it sure as hell beats getting rained on."

Tubar watched the carriage pull away with two more customers. Then eyeballed the inside of the building. The waiting room was lined with wooden benches, and lighted by oil lamps. A pot-bellied stove would keep it warm during cold winter months. The place was near over-flowing with people. With several different languages being spoken. These were foreigners . . . with many dressed in strange European costumes. And through an open doorway he could see into the eating house.

A man, watching them from behind a counter in the waiting room, was wearing a fancy garter above each sleeve-covered elbow. A large gold railroad watch attached to a fat gold chain across his middle, and a paper eyeshade made up the rest of his outfit. He was the station agent.

And Tubar made a bee-line for him. "When does the next coach-train leave for St. Louis?"

The agent studied his watch. "In exactly one hour and nine minutes, son! The trip takes five days, and the train travels at sixteen miles an hour! Do you want one-way or a round-trip ticket, and how many in your party?"

"One way . . . and there are two of us!" Tubar answered. "Do we have time to eat?"

The agent shook his head. "Nope . . . but they'll pack you a lunch basket for fifty cents!" He pointed in the direction of the restaurant.

Tubar pulled the pouch of gold money from his pocket. Opened it and handed Bill twenty dollars. "You buy the food, and I'll take care of the tickets!"

"Don't be flashing that kind of money around, son!" The agent warned, and ran his eyes over Tubar's stout frame. Then stopped on the younger man's battered face. "Thieves work our trains! But maybe you can take care of yourself! Now tell me if you want first or second class!"

"Make it second class!" Tubar answered, and was conserving his funds.

"That will be thirty-five dollars for each of you! Boarding time is in fifteen minutes! I recommend you head straight for the last coach now! And sit at the rear of the car! There'll be less smoke and cinders!"

Tubar handed the agent four Double-Eagles, accepted the tickets, and a ten-dollar gold piece in change. Then thanked the man for his advice, and turned to look for Bill. That one was coming out of the restaurant and was carrying two packages. They met near the doorway leading to the tracks.

"The agent says we should board now," Tubar said. "And sit at the rear of the last car!"

"That's some damn good advice!" Bill replied. "I was sitting closer to the engine on my ride out here. Several hombres and I did a lot of crying!"

Tubar laughed, knowing they were hopping freights, and led the way to the last coach in the train. Then stepped aside to allow Bill to board first, He followed him into the car. They would be far away from the engine's stack, open tender, and the U.S. Mail Car.

"Damn! This is going to get us to St. Louis in a hurry!" Bill exclaimed, and seated himself on the right side of the aisle. He placed his bedroll under the seat, the lunch baskets went onto his lap, and he pulled Tubar's change from a right shirt pocket.

The younger man stopped him with a raised left hand. "Keep it! We'll need more food on the way . . . and I don't want you spending the rest of your money!"

Bill stared at Tubar for a moment. Then at the money. He put it in his right trouser pocket. And handed Tubar one of the baskets.

But they started on the remainder of the cheese and bread first. This was done in silence. Tubar waited until Bill finished eating, and had fished a new sack of Bull Durham smoking tobacco out of his left shirt pocket. Rolled and fired a cigarette. Then the younger man shoved his valise under the seat, and spoke about something that was troubling him.

"I hope giving you money didn't offend you!"

"No!" Bill replied, shaking his head. "It's what I expected you to do!" And he continued in a husky voice. "Team-up with me, Tubar! Let's be partners . . . in everything except women!" Bill grinned when Tubar did. "You do like women . . . don't you?"

"Hell yes! I drink a little too!" And Tubar offered his right hand. "Let's shake on a long friendship!" He continued when Bill released his hand. "Now tell me where we're going!"

"To St. Louis first! To pickup my horse. . . and to outfit you!" Bill took a long drag on his cigarette. "Then we're heading for Dodge City! It's in the State of Kansas!" But he didn't say why they were going there.

Three men entered the car from the front. They seated themselves at that end of the coach. More people . . . men, women and children began filling the remaining seats until all of them were occupied. With Bill running his eyes over each of them. And he continued to Tubar, while pulling his bedroll from under the seat. "Stick that Colt .40 under your belt, and have your shooting paraphernalia where it can be found in a hurry!"

Tubar dragged his valise into the open. Then reached for the revolver. It went under his belt . . . in front of him. Then he watched Bill buckle on a gunbelt, and tie the holster to his right thigh. The pistol in the holster was a Colt Frontier single action .44-40. The gunbelt was lined with loops holding shells.

"Do you have a .44-40 Winchester rifle too?"

Bill pulled the Colt halfway out of the holster. Then eased it back in. To make certain it would come out smooth and easy. And nodded his head. "I have a spare Colt and gunbelt in St. Louis that you can have! But we'll have to buy you a rifle!"

"The agent informed me that thieves ride these trains!" Tubar added. "Only one of us can sleep at a time!"

Bill laughed. "You're going to make a damn good partner!"

* * * *

A long steady blast on the engine's whistle was the driver's signal that it was nearing time for the train to pull away from the depot. And a warning for people to clear the tracks. This increased the excitement felt by many seated in the coach, and had them looking out the windows. Then there was a series of short blasts. The coach jerked forward and began to slowly pick up speed.

Tubar studied the people seated in front of him. They were beginning to settle down. With several watching the three men at the front of the car. And occasionally turning to suspiciously eyeball them.

"They must feel like corralled sheep about now!" Bill observed, noting what his partner was doing. "All these foreigners want is a safe place to hang their hat . . . and something to rest their head on! But many of them have been lied-to and stolen from!"

"Do you expect any trouble?"

"If there is trouble . . . it'll come from those three bastards up front! One of them has been sipping 'shine since they came in!"

Then the Conductor came into the coach. He punched the three men's tickets first. And leaned over to speak to the one who was boozing. The B&O employee worked his way to the rear of the car.

"Are you with them?" He asked, and reached for the tickets Tubar was holding.

"No sir! Are their tickets one-way?"

The Conductor returned the punched tickets to Tubar. Then looked past him. At the gunbelt Bill was wearing. "They have round-trips, and only ride coaches filled with these foreigners!" The ticket-puncher turned to leave. "And I can't stay back here to watch them!"

Tubar looked down at his big hands. Flexed his fingers, and balled them into tight fists. The left hand was slightly swollen from his recent fight.

The train came to a small town. And with several whistle blasts, the driver stopped the engine just beyond a depot. Passengers and freight were dropped off . . . and more travellers and freight were picked up. This process would continue all the way to St. Louis, and on the return trip!

Then dusk was upon the land. And the next stop was longer. Here people and freight were again unloaded, and loaded. As well as a supply of wood for the tender, and water for the engine.

The train was once again moving. With the clicking of so many wheels over rail-joints, lulling some of the people to sleep. But Tubar saw that they too were taking turns at napping.

And the Conductor returned to light a lamp at each end of the coach. As before, he paused to say something to the passenger that was hitting the 'shine too hard.

"HELL!" The passenger yelled. "I'm not bothering anyone! Am I, fellows?" This appeal for assistance was to his companions. It silenced the entire car.

The Conductor stood his ground. "I don't want any trouble! Don't start any . . . if you want to ride my train back to Grafton!"

Laughter followed the Conductor out of the car. And the nearly drunk passenger rose to his feet. Then weaved along the aisle. The man, ignoring the men, boldly undressed each woman he came to with his eyes. He arrived at the rear of the car, turned, and started back. To stop beside a young blonde-headed woman.

"I like you! Even if you are a damn foreigner!" And the fellow reached for the nearest breast with his right hand, The frightened woman screamed.

Tubar was out of his seat and moving toward the man like a big cat. He grabbed the hand just as it touched the woman. "You bastard!" Tubar growled. "Try handling this!"

A hard right fist, slamming into the drinker's stomach, lifted him off his feet. Tubar's left sent the man sliding on his back. To stop beside his companions. Who were now on their feet.

One of them moved into the aisle and faced Tubar. His eyes were on the pistol in the younger man's belt. "I hope you know how to use that, boy!"

Several loud clicks had the man looking past Tubar. They were made by the cocking of a Colt .44-40. "My partner doesn't play that game yet!" Bill's deep voice said. "He does our fist-fighting, and I do our gunfighting! Now . . . right easy like! Pull your pistols out with two fingers and place them on the floor!"

Bill waiting until two big revolvers were laying on the floor. Then spoke to Tubar. "Search your sleeping friend and see what he's packing!"

Tubar moved to where the man was lying. Who was still unconscious. And ran his hands over the still form until finding another Colt. Tubar turned to show it to Bill, and let his eyes stop on the woman's face. Her eyes still showed fear. But she was smiling at him,

"See what else he has!" Bill instructed, from behind Tubar. And moved so that he was facing the standing men. "Step out to the platform, gentlemen!" Such was his order. Bill trailed them out of the car, and returned alone.

"This one has over a hundred dollars!" Tubar said, and was holding a fist-full of gold and paper money.

"That feel is going to cost the son of a bitch!" Bill added, and reached for the money. "Throw him off the train too!"

Tubar turned his victim over. This put him on his stomach. And a strong right hand grabbed the man's belt. Then carried him out to the platform. One hard swing had a tangle of arms and legs disappearing into the night. "Bye . . . bye!" Tubar said, waved, and went back inside the coach.

The remaining passengers were still silent. But were now looking at him and Bill with friendly . . . trusting eyes. And Tubar, on his way to his seat, was approaching the blonde-headed woman.

She reached for his right hand, and stopped his progress. "I thank you!" Her words were in halting American.

Tubar squeezed her hand. Then released it. "I'm glad my partner and I were here! Tell these people they can rest now! Those men won't be coming back!"

"I think she likes you!" A grinning Bill remarked, when the younger man was back in his seat.

"That drunk has good taste!" And Tubar continued. "What did you do with the money?" He could see the pistols. They were laying on Bill's lap.

"I gave it to her! And we have three damn good Colts! You get two of them . . . and we'll sell the third!"

Tubar thought of the five-shot .40 that Master Schieman had placed in his valise. "I'll keep my old Colt! A good friend gave it to me! Along with this money!"

Bill nodded his head. "Then carry it in the bag for an emergency! Which ones of these do you want?"

"Hell . . . I don't know much about pistols!"

The older man laughed. And handed Tubar one of the revolvers. "This pistol has the best feeling action and balance! It's the one you'll pack in a holster!" Bill watched Tubar place the old .40 in the valise, and push the .44-40 under his belt. "And this spare goes in the valise too! The money those bastards saved us will buy you a good horse and gear!"

Three

The solid bay gelding was saddled and tethered to the corral fence behind a trading post. Alongside Bill's saddled gray gelding, and a loaded sorrel packhorse. Even it was a gelding. Bill didn't want a mare along that would be coming in season every eighteen days.

Tubar, who was now looking like a cowhand in his new outfit, and less like a greenhorn, removed his new John B. hat. Then wiped beads of sweat from his forehead with a large green bandanna. He shoved the bandanna deep into his left rear trouser pocket. And dropped his right hand onto the butt of the Colt he was packing. Like Bill's, the holster was tied to his right thigh. A long-bladed skinning knife was sheathed at his left hip.

He eyeballed his gear. The double-rigged Texas saddle; rifle boot and the Winchester stock sticking out of it; full saddlebags; a large canteen hanging from each side of the saddle horn; bedroll; coat and slicker tied on top of the latter. He even owned a pair of moccasins and gloves now.

Tubar glanced down at his new boots. Now dusty due to a long walk in the corral. While following Bill . . . as he selected a strong mount for his younger partner. An eight year old, sixteen hands, well-trained, disciplined sound gelding took his fancy. The lone previous owner was said to be a woman.

The new owner was standing behind the horse and off to one side. The big critter was flicking its ears back and forth while watching its new Master. Tubar was wondering if the horse were a kicker. The distance he was maintaining between him and its hind legs . . . was one of caution and respect.

And Tubar walked back and forth behind the gelding. With his spurs a-jingling. The purpose was to get the horse used to the sound. To associate it with him.

Then he went to the gelding. Placed his right hand on its left hip, and walked to the fence. Tubar rubbed the horse's shoulder, per Bill's instructions. The mount smelled of its new Master, blew through its nostrils, and began rubbing Tubar's left shoulder with its broad upper lip. A beginning of deep trust between animal and Master.

Tubar scratched the gelding's left ear. While thinking of the paraphernalia in his saddlebags. The right bag contained his Colt .40; three boxes of shells; and tools to care for his mounts hoofs. The left bag was full of jerky. And the spare .44-40 pistol was in his bedroll.

Then he thought of the money he'd spent. The amount he had remaining was a little over one hundred twenty dollars. But he owned his horse and gear . . . as his partner did. Bill said they'd find work on a spread near Dodge City.

Tubar walked away from his mount. Turned and looked at the animal. A strong horse . . . for a big rider.

"Have you named him yet, partner?"

Tubar turned at the sound of Bill's voice. "What was that Spanish word you used when we first met? I liked the sound of it!"

"Was it . . . hombre? That means . . . man!" The older partner watched Tubar shake his head. "Hell! It must have been . . . Amigo! That means . . . friend!"

"It's the word!" Tubar exclaimed. "I'll call him . . . Amigo!"

Bill laughed. "That's not a bad name for a horse your future will be depending on!" And he continued. "We have a job on a wagon train headed for the Santa Fe trail! It pulls out early in the morning!"

"What kind of a wagon train?"

"Freight wagons, and some settlers! The bigger the train, the less trouble we'll have!"

"Are you talking about Indians?"

"Yep!" And Bill grinned. "Plus four and two-legged varmints!"

Tubar thought of the few Indians he'd seen here in St. Louis. None of them were carrying weapons. Not even a knife. "Now tell me what our job will be!"

"Guards! We'll be working at night! After the wagons are circled!" Then Bill continued. "We need to get to the outfit too! The owner of twenty freight wagons wants us to start tonight!"

Tubar untied Amigo's reins. Placed his left boot in the stirrup and swung into the saddle. He backed the horse away from the fence. Then watched Bill climb into his saddle. He was holding the packhorse's lead-rope.

"How long will it take us to get to Dodge City?" Tubar asked, as they rode away from the trading post.

"Almost two months! That Santa Fe trail will be hot as hell when they get past the turn-off to Chouteau's Island! I sure don't envy some of the people!"

"What are the Indians out there called?"

Bill looked at his young partner and grinned. "Comanches and Arapahos! They'd sure like to lift your red hair!" And he continued. "We won't need to worry about raiding parties until we pass Fort Zarah!"

"And they have troops there?"

"Nope . . . the cavalry pulled-out last year!"

Tubar knew that Bill was having fun at his expense. And hit him with another question. "When do you begin teaching me that new way to shoot a pistol?"

"You start working on your draw tonight! The shooting will come later!"

"I'm a good shot with a rifle, Bill! But I'll have to sight this one in!" And Tubar kept talking. "What direction is the wagon train headed in?" They had arrived at the edge of St. Louis.

"West . . . straight as the crow flies! Across Missouri to Independence! Then into Kansas!"

"What kind of a place is this Dodge City?" Tubar asked, as he spotted the first wagon. It was at the end of the line. There were so many . . . the lead wagon in the train wasn't in sight. And they were on the crest of a hill.

"Wild and wooly!" Bill said, answering his question. "But a lot of nice people live there! It's like living in two towns! With a narrow line separating the good and the bad!"

"Jesus Christ!" Tubar exclaimed, and was counting the outfits he could see. "How many wagons are there?"

"Our boss . . . Ben Sprag, says the Wagon Master will be leading over a hundred out of here! And all of them aren't going by way of Santa Fe! Most of the wagons are heading for the gold fields in Colorado!"

Tubar and Bill came to the last wagon. Then continued on in the direction of the front of the line. Bill was looking for Ben Sprag and his freighting outfit. Tubar, with his youthful curiosity running strong, was eyeing each wagon. The teams were made-up of mules, oxen and horses. And darkness was about an hour away. It was Tuesday, May the twenty-first, 1872, and the five-days train ride from Grafton ended early this morning.

* * * *

Bill spotted the first of Ben Sprag's twenty freight wagons. The huge fourteen feet long prairie schooners were painted blue and red. The wheels red . . . and the body blue. With the owner's name painted in large letters on the wagon covers.

The freight wagons were near the head of the line, and Bill knew that nearby was a passel of mules. It would take eight to ten mules to pull the heavy schooners. With some hauling loads weighing up to seven thousand pounds. The teams and freight, would be a real prize to Indians and renegades.

He glanced at Tubar. Several days had gone by since the brawl at The Sailor's Cove, and the swelling was gone from his face. The once dark colored bruises were now turning yellow. Tubar was healing . . . and his movements showed no stiffness.

And Bill located Ben Sprag. Himself a large man, and he had been informed that Tubar would arrive slightly damaged. The older partner headed to where their new boss was inspecting a wagon wheel.

"Here we are, Ben!" Bill said, when the Freighter heard their horses and turned around. "I said we'd be here before nightfall!"

Ben nodded his head, and shook hands with Bill. "Then ten dollars a day and found is agreeable to you?"

Bill glanced at Tubar. "That sounds good to us! And we'll stick with you as far as Dodge City!" Then he continued. "Ben Sprag . . . meet Tubar Lane!"

Ben walked to where Tubar was standing his horse. Grinned, and stuck out his right hand. "Glad to meet you, son! Both of you climb down! And I want your gear in this end wagon! That way the thieves back there will have to come by you . . . to get at my property!"

Tubar shook the hand, grinned back at the big man, and stepped out of the saddle. "We're ready to go to work, sir!"

"That's what I wanted to hear!" And Ben surveyed the part of the wagon train in sight. The wagons were already lined-up in the order they'd roll-out in. "We won't have a lot of stock stealing on the trail! Because the wagons will be circled . . . and my mules and saddle-horses will be inside the circle! But keep an eye on my stock tonight! Each driver will take care of his wagon!" And Ben continued. "You're too damn young and strong for me to whip, son! So . . . please, don't start off by calling me . . . sir!"

The look on Tubar's face made Bill laugh. "I had to insist he stop calling me that too! But I didn't use the same words! I know damn well he can kick my butt!" Then Bill paused for a moment, "Who'll be watching your stock while they're being grazed away from the wagon train?"

"An army of drovers! The Wagon Master will assign permanent jobs to the people here! But not to my drivers and guards!"

Bill nodded his head. And turned to Tubar. "Let's unload the packhorse! Then strip the extra gear off our mounts! The packhorse can be turned loose with the stock at night! But he'll be tied to the wagon during the daytime!"

Tubar ground-reined Amigo, and tied the sorrel to the wagon's tailboard, Then began untying their supplies from the pack-saddle. He stored packsaddle and supplies in the schooner.

And Bill's Gray laid its ears back the very moment Tubar started toward its rear end. This had him approaching the gelding from the side, and talking to it. "Steady now, dammit!" He said in a low soothing voice, "I'm just going to lighten your load!" Tubar untied everything from behind the saddle except the saddlebags. Bedroll, coat, slicker, and one canteen went into the wagon. Then he took the same items off Amigo.

"By God!" Bill exclaimed, when he stopped talking to Ben Sprag, and saw that his young partner had all of their gear stashed. "You're handy as hell!" He reached into his left saddlebag and came out with a handful of dried meat. Then gave half of it to Tubar. "Let's go see what Ben's horses and mules look like! In case one gets stolen!"

* * * *

A quarter-moon was lighting the lush grass and weed covered

terrain about two miles west of St. Louis. The first hour of darkness was past, and one could now see about. Each team of mules, numbering ten, were tethered to the wagon they'd be harnessed to. And the same critters would always be hitched to the same wagon . . . and they'd always be trailing the same wagon.

Tubar and Bill made their first round afoot, and introduced themselves to each of the drivers. The lines, at the wagon their gear was stored in, would be handled by an hombre some older than Bill. Who had said his age was about forty years. And the driver's name was Tommy Bayes. Who fought with the Texas Brigade and was damn proud of it. This was said between squirts of tobacco spit, and Tommy had already spotted Tubar as a damn Yankee. But he wouldn't hold that against the younger man . . . if he came to like him.

Bill and Tubar returned to the last freight wagon. Where Bill listened to the noise of animal sounds, and people talking, from in front and behind them.

"The wagon train will keep moving from sunup to sundown every day." Bill explained. "And the members' will settle down about the same time each night! No Indian or renegade in his right mind is going to mess around here when they're up! There are too damn many guns . . . and people who'll shoot at anything that doesn't look or sound right!"

"Will they be like that all the time?"

"Nope! Most will get over this when they become trail-wise! The point I'm making . . . is that you'll be able to practice drawing that Colt before these people turn-in for the night! Now watch my right hand!"

Tubar looked down just as it moved, and found himself staring into the business end of Bill's .44-40. "Damn! How'd you do that?"

"By practicing for more hours than I care to count! Now unload yours!" Bill waited until this was done. "Ease it back into the holster, so it will slide out easy! Now . . . we don't want any wasted motion! Drop your hand until it's just below the butt! That's good!" And he continued. "You want to bring your hand up in one smooth motion, and the Colt comes up with it! Once you learn when the barrel clears leather, bend your wrist and elbow until the barrel is pointing at your target!"

Tubar raised his right hand and felt his fingers close around the handle of the pistol. He kept bringing the hand up. Then tried to swing the barrel forward. It didn't clear the holster.

"Don't let that bother you!" The older man encouraged. "You'll get better! And when you can clear leather without thinking about it, start pulling the hammer and trigger back at the same time! It's all in the timing! You want to be shooting the very instant you line-up on your target!"

"But when do I aim this damn thing?"

"You don't aim the damn thing!" Bill answered. "You point it from waist high! We'll leave the wagon every day so you can do some still target shooting!"

"That's going to take a hell of a lot of shells! And I only have three boxes!"

"I bought ten extra boxes! They're with the supplies!"

Tubar practiced his draw without noticeable results. And when the wagon train members started turning-in, he reloaded the Colt. Then began leading Amigo. As he patrolled the right side of the wagons. Bill was waiting for him at the front schooner.

"We'll work in pairs for awhile, Tubar! Then separate! And change directions often! Don't set a pattern!"

"Do I stay on this side when we split-up?"

"Yep . . . so the stock will get use to seeing you and Amigo over here! And keep one eye on his head! He'll see and hear things you won't! It'll help keep you alive!" Then Bill continued. "Another thing . . . pay attention to night sounds! When the little critters' stop making noise, something unusual has disturbed them!"

Tubar reversed his direction. While thinking about what Bill told him. He glanced at Amigo's head. The big horse was looking at the nearest team. Then Tubar turned his attention to the sounds away from the wagon. He could hear a night-bird, several crickets, and a lone coyote yipping in the distance. Something was disturbing the leaves under a nearby bush. These were sounds he'd ignored before . . . but were now an ally.

* * * *

The heavy Winchester .44-40 bucked hard against Tubar's right shoulder. And dust boiled-up above a small rock. "It's shooting high! I'll lower the rear sight!"

Bill watched the shooter miss the rock again. But the lead bullet must have come within an eyelash of it. "Bring it down another notch! Until the rock is on top of your front sight! That way our rifles will shoot the same!"

Tubar lowered the rear sight once more. Jacked another shell into the firing chamber, aimed at the same rock, pulled the trigger, and grinned when the target exploded. "By hell, Bill! This thing shoots good!"

"Let me try it!" Bill took the rifle and levered a shell into the chamber. Aimed at a second rock and pulled the trigger. The rock burst into dozens of pieces. And he nodded his satisfaction. "The only difference between this rifle and mine is the trigger pull! I can live with that! Let's get closer and see what you can do with your Colt!"

Bill reloaded Tubar's rifle. Pushed it into the boot, and led their mounts closer to the hill they were shooting into. Then watched his partner draw and fire the revolver. The bullet missed its target by five feet. Bill busted out laughing.

"That bad . . . huh!"

"Nope! It made me think of myself! But you'll get better! One day that .44-40 will come out of the holster like it's part of your arm! Then you'll have . . ." Bill stopped talking when he saw that Tubar was watching the horses. The horses, both used to gunshots, had spotted something on a hill that was directly behind them.

"It can't be a deer!" Tubar said, and moved to place his mount between him and the hill. He holstered the Colt and pulled the rifle from the boot. "A deer would lie still . . . or already be gone!"

Bill grinned, and was also behind the Gray. "Some bastard is watching us! And I doubt that it's an Indian!"

"Do you want to flush him out?"

The older, more experienced man shook his head. "Nope, that would be playing his game! Let's lead our horses to the far side of this hill, and catch the wagon train! You'll practice more tomorrow!"

They led the Gray and Bay around the base of the hill. Then mounted and urged them into a running-walk. Once the horses were warm, Bill touched his mount in the flanks with his spurs. The Gray increased his gait to a swinging lope. And Tubar's Bay stayed with him.

The hot Sunday afternoon was almost gone when the last wagon was sighted. Bill and Tubar slowed their mounts to a walk. So they would cool slowly. Even then the fast walking horses were covering ground faster than the teams. The wagons were being passed one by one.

"Some of these people look like the foreigners who boarded the train at Grafton with us!" Bill commented.

"I was thinking the same thing! I know damn well I saw that man and woman at the depot!" Tubar said, as they came to another wagon. "They're wearing the same clothing too!"

"Damn! They must have brought some money over here! Those traders in St. Louis don't give these outfits away!" The wagons the foreigners were driving were all conestogas . . . and being pulled by big conestoga horses.

Tubar twisted in his saddle so he could look into the wagon they were passing. "They had to be carrying gold! And . . . all of these children can't have the same mother and father!"

"Maybe they're related, and were carrying part of the family fortune! But I've always heard these people were as poor as church mice!"

Tubar laughed as he glanced at Bill. "Most of them are!" Then he swung his eyes back to the moving wagons. They locked onto another pair of eyes. "O boy," he continued, "there she is!"

Bill had spotted the blonde-headed woman too. "Just remember to get home before dark, partner!" And laughing, he rode on.

Tubar reined to the walking woman. Dismounted and began pacing her, while leading Amigo. "I wondered if I would see you again!"

"I saw you pass last night before dark! I saw you ride by this morning!"

He looked into her eyes. Eyes that were a deeper blue than his, "I hope walking with you isn't going to make someone mad at me!"

"I am not taken . . . or promised! If that is what you are seeking to learn!"

Tubar grinned, and watched a smile form on her lips. "My name is Tubar Lane!"

"And mine is Ingrid Johansen! My Mother and Father are watching us from the far side of this wagon!"

"Do you have any brothers and sisters!" Tubar asked, and judged her to be at least five-feet ten. Without the heavy walking shoes she was wearing.

Ingrid held three fingers up for Tubar to see. "They're all older brothers! And watching us too!" Then she smiled again. "Where are you going, Tubar Lane?"

"Dodge City! My partner and I are going to work there!"

"What kind of work will you be doing?"

"Bill works with cattle! He's a cowhand!" Tubar paused a moment before continuing. "I was to be a bookkeeper in my Father's business! But something went wrong at school . . . and the Chancellor bounced me!"

"Is that what happened to your face?"

Tubar grinned at her. While nodding his head. "I was obtaining some information from a bartender at a tavern! And a bunch of his customers didn't like the way I was doing it!" Then Tubar glanced at the sun. It was almost to the horizon. "I work for Ben Sprag as a night guard! My partner is waiting for me!"

"Then you must go!"

Tubar nodded his head. Then climbed into the saddle. "It was nice seeing you again!"

He squeezed Amigo with his legs and the Bay went into a ground-covering running-walk. His thoughts were on Ingrid Johansen. Her people were in five conestoga wagons. Tubar wondered again if they were all related, and where they were headed to.

Then he began thinking of the life he ran from. But in reality, it ended when Chancellor McElroy expelled him. Tubar finally decided he hadn't wanted to be a bookkeeper in his Father's damn business.

Four

The wagon train had rolled away from St. Louis on a rutted, heavily used road. Trees and large bushes on each side of the road had been cut for firewood by so many trains that a swath four-miles wide was cleared. With the road running through the middle of it.

Huge campsites, where wagon trains had circled many times before, were each Wagon Master's daily objective. For those who could reach them. They were located about fifteen miles apart. Such a place had been reached by this wagon train.

The wagons were circled under the watchful eye of the Wagon Master. A task that in time would become routine to all the drivers. When this was accomplished, he called his first meeting. One that Ben Sprag's employees, and those of other Freighters', were not required to attend.

Men were assigned as drovers, night guards and meat hunters. The Wagon Master's word was the only law on the trail, and the jobs would last throughout the long journey. The responsibility of taking care of the injured and sick, making fires, and cooking, was assigned to the women.

He informed the members the wagons would be circled each night. And the stock allowed to graze until midnight. Then brought inside the protective wall of wagons.

* * * *

A disappearing moon welcomed the people when the meeting ended. And each began the task assigned to him or her. Oxen, horses and mules were gathered by the drovers, and taken beyond the circle. Guards were riding outside the circle, and fires were being made. Soon the aroma of cooking meat and beans was wafting among the wagons. And Tubar eyed the fire that Tommy Bayes was tending. His stomach was growling like a bad thunderstorm when Bill showed up leading his

Gray. "I hope Tommy likes me tonight! I'm getting hungry enough to bite Amigo here!"

Bill laughed. "I'll bet that big devil could really unwind . . . when he gets mad!" And Bill continued. "Maybe that pretty blonde will feed you! If she can cook!"

Tubar grinned. "She showed me her mother and father!"

"Did you meet them?"

"Hell no! But the opening was there!"

"Why didn't you take it?"

"Those people have a code of their own! Girl asks boy if he wants to meet parents! And if boy says yes . . . and parents like boy . . . boy is a cooked goose!"

"Well, if you don't want her! Some lucky bastard will! She's one hell of a woman!"

They had arrived at the lead freight wagon. And began the long walk back to the end. Bill continued talking. "We'll have to mind our business when this place quietens down! But that won't happen until the drovers turn-in!"

"Do you figure Tommy will feed us?"

"He will me! But you're a damn Yankee!" And Bill busted out laughing. "No . . . the drivers will feed us! But Ben wants us to eat with a different one each night! Tommy's waiting for us now!"

* * * *

Tubar's horse heard the stock returning before he did. A big hole in the circle was waiting for them. And was closed when every head was inside. Soon after the stocks arrival the wagon train was quiet.

The night critters began making noise again. These sounds Tubar was listening to, and occasionally glancing at Amigo's head.

Tubar was walking. With the Bay alongside of him. The big horse had its muzzle touching its Master's right shoulder. Each time Amigo moved his head, Tubar would stop and look in the same direction. The darkening hours wore on.

And about the time Tubar decided the night would pass quietly, heavy gunfire could be heard from the far side of the circle. Tubar was looking in that direction, as most all the people would be. Then the youngster glanced at Amigo's head again. The horse was looking at something on their side, and behind them.

Tubar looped the split-rein around Amigo's neck, and slapped him on the rump. "Go, dammit!" He ordered in a low voice, and the Bay continued on. Then Tubar cat-footed to the nearest schooner, and made his way back to a position he felt would be in the path of anyone coming toward the wagons.

He dropped to his hands and knees, and backed under the wagon like a crawdad running from a hungry catfish. Then lay on his stomach. Tubar drew his Colt, while wishing Bill was here, and that he'd remembered to grab his rifle.

The shooting was still heavy. With Tubar trying to shut it out of his mind. He was looking to each side of him, when several dark forms rose from the ground and made a run for the wagon he was under.

Tubar aimed his revolver at the nearest man and pulled the trigger. The heavy pistol jumped upward, and the bullet slammed the man onto his back. He squeezed one more shot off, before realizing they were backing up and shooting at him. Lead bullets were ripping long slivers out of the wooden side of the schooner, and whining as they ricocheted off metal rims.

Then the hammer struck a spent shell. Tubar hurriedly reloaded the Colt, and strained to see into the night. But there was no movement in front of him now. He continued to lay under the wagon. And the shooting stopped on the far side of the circle. Still Tubar didn't move.

"It was a blasted trick!" Ben yelled, from near the wagon Tubar was under. "Who did the shooting?"

"It wasn't me!" The driver answered. "But this schooner took several bullets! I heard them hitting the side!"

"Son of a bitch! Here's that big Bay . . . standing alone! They got Tubar!"

"Dammit! I was coming to like that Yankee!" Tommy Bayes added. "Now I can't tell him!"

"That's not a very respectful position to shoot a pistol from!" A deep voice said from behind Tubar.

"Maybe not! But it kept me alive!"

"Are you hurt?" Bill continued, as he crawled under the wagon.

"Nope . . . but I was scared to death! I just stopped shaking!"

"You did real fine! How many shots did you get off?"

"Five . . . and I remembered to reload!"

"Did you hit any of them?" Bill asked.

"Two for sure! They're still out there!"

"Well . . . their bastard partners are gone! Let's get some men and lanterns, and see what we can find!"

Tubar and Bill crawled from under the schooner. Tommy was the first to see them.

"TUBAR!" He yelled. "You're not dead?"

"Hell no! And you're a disgrace to the South!" This started several of the other drivers laughing.

"I may be, son! But I'm glad you're alive and walking!"

"Did you do all that shooting on this side?" Ben asked Tubar.

"Yes . . . and my horse spotted them for me!"

"Where were they?"

"On the far side of this wagon!" Bill answered for his partner. "Get some lanterns and we'll have a look!"

A small army of heavily armed men left the circle. With some holding lit oil lanterns above their head. Ben Sprag found the first dead man.

"This one is in hell!" He said. "And bored dead center! Take everything worth having! It goes to Tubar!"

"Here's number two and three!" Tommy added. "And another unlucky renegade left with blood pouring out of his ass! Damn, Tubar," he continued, "you're plumb mean with that Colt!"

Tubar, still holding his pistol, walked to where Ben found the first renegade. And stared down at the dead man.

Bill took the gun from his partner's hand, and dropped it back into the holster. "A man kills to protect himself and others! But this part never gets easy!"

Tubar nodded his agreement. Then walked to where Amigo was being held.

* * * *

The weapons carried by the renegades now had new owners. Three gunbelts and revolvers. Two were Colt .44-40s, which Bill immediately sold. The third, a Baby Dragoon Colt, was given to Tommy by Tubar. And the dead men's horses had been appropriated by their companions.

At the first light of the new day, with the wagon train fairly buzzing with talk of the attack, the Wagon Master gave the order to "roll the wagons!" The order was passed along from driver to driver. And as a wagon arrived where the dead men lay unburied, each member came to understand some of the dangers they would face in the land to the west.

During the following trouble-free nineteen days the Wagon Master led his charges in a western direction. The route meandered among grass covered hills dotted with bushes and trees. The latter were getting smaller . . . except near water . . . and less in number. But there was still an abundance of forage for the stock.

The members were now seasoned walkers, and trail-wise. Mules, horses and oxen, whether being ridden or pulling loaded wagons, were trail-tough.

Arrow Rock was the first hint that the wagon train was entering a different world. Then long abandoned Fort Osage, established in 1808, for the purpose of keeping a watchful eye on what moved on the Missouri River and controlling the Iowa, Osage and Kansa Indians, was reached.

And after twenty hot days on the trail, on Monday, June the tenth, 1872, the wagon train arrived at Independence. The wagons were circled near the frontier town. With the Wagon Master informing the members they had two days to make repairs, rest their stock, and to replenish supplies. This resulted in a bunch of people heading for the trading posts. Of the number were Bill and Tubar.

The trading post they entered was in a long building. With a warehouse in the rear, and a corral back of that. A man could buy horses; mules; burros; oxen; axes; shovels; food staples; calico cloth; pistols; rifles; brooms; handmade clothing; handles; lead; powder and shells. Rope; bull-whips; bridles and other paraphernalia hung from the rafters overhead.

Tubar ran his eyes over the merchandise. Then nodded his head. "We can buy what we need in this one place! But first I want a bath and haircut." He fingered the growth of beard on his face. "And maybe a shave."

"I saw a bathhouse across the road from here!" Bill added. "Let's head for it!"

It was but an hour later when they emerged from the bathhouse. The dirt and horse-smell was gone, hair cut back, and both of them had been shaved. Or almost shaved. Bill looked his young partner over.

"I'm glad you decided to keep that red mustache. It makes you look older! And you're a sight more grown-up now!"

Tubar ran his fingers over the hair still on his upper lip. "I'll have to keep the damn thing trimmed too!"

"Get that pretty blonde to do it!"

"I've only been close enough to wave at her!" And Tubar ignored Bill's poking fun at him. Then he spotted a nearby tavern. "I haven't had a drink of ale in weeks! I want to see what that tavern looks like on the inside too!"

Bill had to grin. "That's a damn saloon . . . out here! And don't you dare order ale! We call it . . . beer!"

They glanced at their mounts which were tethered in front of the trading post. Then walked to the saloon. To find a long bar lined with men from the wagon train. Tubar and Bill joined them.

"What will you have?" A bartender asked Bill.

"Do you have any of that Mexican tequila?" Bill answered, while running his eyes over a line of bottled spirits sitting on a long shelf behind the man.

"We sure as hell do! The road from Mexico goes right by this place!"

"Pour me a shot . . . and my partner wants a beer!"

A clear liquid was measured into a shot-glass for Bill, and a beer was drawn for Tubar. "That will be fifty cents."

Tubar placed a half-dollar shin plaster on the bar. Then followed Bill to a vacant table. He took a long drink, and wiped foam off his mouth with the back of his left hand. "Damn. That tastes good!"

"Now that you've lost your baby-fat, how much do you figure you weigh?"

Tubar grinned, and looked at his arms. "At least two hundred pounds . . . and it wasn't baby-fat! I've been eating different kinds of . . . ."

"AT LEAST BUY A LADY A DRINK!"

The loud voice was at the bar. It came from one of the saloon girls. A slender woman, with long hair that was neither blonde nor red. And she was yelling at one of the younger men in Ingrid's group.

"Hell," she continued, "he can't even understand me!"

"Maybe he doesn't want to go to bed with you!" Tubar said from where he was sitting. "Maybe he doesn't want to buy you a drink!"

Tubar's voice had the foreigner looking at him. And he backed away from the bar in an attempt to leave. Then three men rose to their feet from a nearby table and blocked his path.

"The lady wants you to buy her a drink, Mister!" The largest of the three said. "We want you to buy her a drink!"

Words were coming out of the foreigner's mouth that couldn't be understood. He was also motioning with his hands. His eyes were on the weapons in the three men's holsters.

"They'll be some of the town's toughs!" Bill said in a low voice to Tubar. "And they most likely work for this place!"

"Cover my back!" Tubar said, and rose to his feet. He walked up behind the man that was doing the talking. Then tapped him on the right shoulder. "He's trying to leave here peacefully, Mister! Let him go!"

"Stay out of this, son of a bitch!"

Tubar slammed his right fist into the man's right kidney. The force of the blow made him scream, and knocked him to his knees. Tubar eased the pistol from his holster and placed it on the bar.

"Let him go!" Tubar repeated to the two men who were now facing him. "Or end up on the floor with your partner!"

They moved to one side, and watched Tubar motion for the strangely dressed foreigner to leave. And kept their eyes on him until he was through the doorway.

"Don't cause him or his people any trouble while we're here!" Bill's deep voice said from behind Tubar. "You do . . . and my sidekick is going to stomp on your ass! If he doesn't . . . I'll shoot big holes in it!"

Tubar watched the two men half-carry their partner to a closed door at the rear of the saloon. Then they were gone too. He returned to his table and sat down. Waited until Bill joined him, picked up his glass of beer, and clicked it against Bill's shot-class. "Do you think they'll come back?"

"If they do . . . this place will get shot all to hell! Every jack-man from the wagon train had his hand on a pistol-butt! They were backing us all the way!"

"Some of Ingrid's people are going to have a rough time making it in this part of the country!" Tubar added.

"Nope . . . all they have to do is learn to talk like me!"

* * * *

The wagon train left Independence on a cloudy, rainy Thursday morning. It was now headed for the Oregon Trail Junction. And Tubar was finally informed by Bill . . . that the day of massive Indian attacks had passed. Thus the closing of Fort Zarah. But he was reminded that on occasions the younger warriors would select them a War Chief and leave the reservations. The wagon train could still be harassed by small bands of Cheyenne and Arapaho.

Bill and Tubar were resting in the rear of Tommy's big prairie schooner. Amigo, the Gray, and the packhorse, were tied to the tailboard of the moving wagon.

"We could have lived in Independence for a month on what money those three renegades had on them!"

Tubar watched rain water run off the cover over them. While thinking about the almost fifty dollars Tommy had brought to him. He split it with Bill. And there were bowie and skinning knives which he gave to the drivers.

"I don't think they liked us there! I'm glad to be back on the trail!"

Bill grinned, and was keeping an eye on the team pulling the schooner following them, "We aren't away from that damn town yet! Those mules' are losing their footing! It's getting slick out there!"

The words were no sooner out of his mouth and the wagon began slowing down. Then it was stopped.

"This is as far as we go until the rain stops!" Tommy said, from the outside, "And I'm soaked to the skin!"

"Do you figure he could use our assistance?" Tubar asked Bill.

"HELL YES, HE CAN!" Tommy yelled. "Give me a hand before one of my mules goes down!"

"That damn Reb has big ears!" Tubar continued, as he climbed out. And pulled his slicker on. He started toward the front, and Amigo nickered his displeasure at being left behind. "Sorry, horse! You can't come along this time!"

They helped Tommy unhitch the teams. Then unhook the mules.

But the harness stayed on. The long-eared critters were tied to the schooner.

And Bill walked away from the wagon. He kicked at the ground. "It's not too wet out here! But so many wheels and hoofs are making that part bad!"

The rainfall slowed in the middle of the afternoon, and the sky cleared. To let a hot drying-sun touch the ground. Tubar and Bill saddled their horses and rode toward the rear of the strung-out wagons. They were seeking a secluded place that would allow Tubar to continue his practice in privacy.

As the members of the wagon train had become accustomed to, the two guards were returning early in the evening. They rode past the same people and by the same wagons. And as on an earlier day, Ingrid was watching them. But this time she was walking to meet Tubar.

And without looking at Bill, Tubar neck-reined Amigo in her direction. Dismounted, and joined her on the ground.

"My brother told us what you did for him! You have assisted us twice now!"

"He must learn the ways of his new people!" Tubar said, while thinking of Bill's words: "Some lucky bastard will grab this woman!" Then he continued to Ingrid. "Most of our people aren't like the woman or those three men! They have forgotten that our ancestors came from someplace else too!" Tubar was now thinking of the Cherokee . . . and The Trail of Tears, that Bill spoke of.

"My Father complained to Rolv about going into such a place!"

Tubar was silent for a moment. While watching her people watch them. "Rolv and most of your other men will go into more places like that for a drink! And there will be other whores in those places! Tell them not to go alone!"

Ingrid nodded her understanding. "You are the one who killed those men!"

Tubar climbed into the saddle. "Yes! I'm the one! They were going to steal from my boss . . . and were trying to kill me!" Then he squeezed Amigo with his legs.

* * * *

Most of one day had been lost because of the wet slick ground. But on the following Friday morning, the Wagon Master again gave the order to "roll the wagons!"

It took the long line of slow moving wagons all of Friday and part of Saturday, to arrive at the trail's junction to Oregon. And in eight days from Independence, after being halted by a huge herd of buffalo, the wagon train was circled on the west side of Council Grove.

This was where the Santa Fe trail began, and the Overland stage run to California. The passengers and mail would arrive in that far land in twenty-five days.

The appearance of Kansas was a drastic change from that of grassy Missouri. From lush green meadows and hills . . . to a sparse brown. There was now short stubby grass for the stock to graze on; and an over-abundance of small cactus plants dotted the terrain. Stories were being told of a long stretch of waterless trail between the Cimarron and Canadian Rivers. And only mules, that could survive on this short grass during hot summer months, stood a chance of making it to Santa Fe. In the Territory of New Mexico. This had many of the people who did not wish to go to Colorado, deciding to settle in or near Dodge City.

And on Sunday morning, June the sixteenth, the wagon train rolled away from Council Grove. Twenty more buffalo plagued days went by. The steady rolling wagons, having to stop seven more times for the herds, crossed the Neosho River; the Arkansas River: passed Abandoned Fort Zarah; Pawnee Rock, and Fort Larned. Then, on a Wednesday, July the tenth, 1872, fifty days after rolling away from St. Louis, the wagons were circled just away from Fort Dodge. Near the junction of the wet and dry routes of the Santa Fe trail.

Five

"I sure wish you boys would stay-on!" Were Ben Sprag's words as he paid-off Bill and Tubar. Ben was headed for the Santa Fe trail. Which would end in the mountain village of Santa Fe. Then the freight wagons would swing to the south. Follow the Rio Grande past several Indian towns; Albuquerque; Socorro; Mesilla; and on to the border town of El Paso. Once called El Paso Del Norte by the Mexicans. "The Pass to the North!" But Tubar and Bill declined Ben's offer. Shook his hand and rode away from the wagon train.

Bill pulled-up a short distance from where Ben was standing. "I strongly doubt we'll see this again!" He said, and pointed at the railroad tracks in front of them. "That's the Atchison, Topeka & Santa Fe! And this most likely will be the last big wagon train that will be formed! At least by Freighters and settlers! The settlers can ride coach-trains now!"

Tubar nodded his agreement. Then wrinkled his nose as a strong odor reached them. "What in the hell is that smell?"

"Drying buffalo hides! That's a booming business in Dodge City! And the reason a lot of people call the place . . . Buffalo City!"

"I don't want that kind of work, Bill! Not after seeing so many decaying carcasses along the trail!"

Bill looked at his younger partner for a moment. "I'm glad you feel that way! I went out with one bunch of buffalo hiders! We were working for a man called Hoodoo Brown! And must have shot three hundred of the big devils the first day! What hides and meat couldn't be brought back . . . were left to rot! The senseless killing made me sick to my stomach!"

"Well . . . let's go! Show me this Dodge City!"

"Not so damn fast!" Bill replied, and kept talking. "You've become pretty slick with that Colt . . . and at throwing a knife! And one day you'll have to use both of them! Just remember to watch the man's eyes! They'll change expression a split-second before he starts his draw! That's when you bust him!"

Bill watched several wagons pull away from the circle, and head for the town. Which was located west of Fort Dodge. He squeezed the Gray with his legs and followed them. But pulled up again when he came to the railroad tracks. He and Tubar were looking into Dodge City.

"This is Front Street . . . facing the tracks!" He Continued. "You can tell which is the tough side!" And he pointed to his left. "There are at least seventeen saloons over here! Plus a tent restaurant; a barber shop; laundries; gambling; and not enough whores to go around! And," he pointed to his right, "there's a nice hotel over here called the . . . Dodge House, with a nice restaurant! A meal costs one dollar! The owner is a woman . . . and she won't allow a whore in the place!"

Tubar laughed. "You're plumb full of information! Keep talking!"

"I've been holding-out on you, partner! There's a reason I brought you to Dodge City!"

Tubar made a restless Amigo stand still. The Bay was getting impatient. "Well . . . hit me with it!"

"There are, or were, several Madams with their own house! One is called . . . Alice; Another is Dutch Kate; Susie's; and Starlet's!"

"Madams!" Tubar exclaimed, while pulling Amigo around so he could look Bill straight in the eye. "What kind of Madams?"

"Hell . . . you know the kind! They have a bunch of girls working for them!"

"Son of a bitch! Are you putting me on," Tubar watched Bill shake his head. "What does she look like?"

"Tall . . . redheaded, and you look like her!"

"My God, Bill! How well do you know this woman?"

"Very well!" And Bill held back a grin. "We're damn good friends! I'm looking forward to seeing her! Just as soon as I wash this horse smell and dirt off!"

"But you can't do that!"

"Why the hell not?"

"Dammit, Bill! You can't go to bed with her! She could be my Mother!"

The older man was watching Tubar's face, "You're serious about this!"

"Hell yes, I'm serious! How would you feel?"

"I don't know! But this Starlet and I have known each other for a long time!"

"It's different now, and . . . what do you mean . . . this Starlet?"

"There are two here! Both redheads, they resemble you . . . and don't like one another worth a damn!"

"Come on now, Bill! There can't be two of them!"

"Partner Tubar, if I'm lying . . . I'm dying! And I'll bet everything I own, that one of them is your Ma!"

"O my God! Two of them!"

"And the tough part is . . . I like Starlet's house better than the others!"

"I don't know if I can go in her place, Bill! What will she think if I turn out to be her son?"

Bill laughed. "That damn sure won't be any worse than her being a Madam!" And he paused for a moment. "I know a way to find out if she's your Ma! But we need to give you a new name!"

"And you've got one in mind?"

"Use the name of that teacher you like! Call yourself . . . Red Schieman!"

Red nodded his agreement. "Where is the other Starlet?"

"She and her husband, Jim Lawson, showed up about two years ago! They own a big ranch south of here . . . the Leaning-S! And they brought two or three youngsters with them!" Then Bill continued. "A man called . . . Hank Sitler, owns another big outfit! It's located to the north and west!"

Bill flicked the Gray's reins. And started him along Front Street. He led his younger partner across the tracks and to a stable. Where they boarded the horses and gear. Then carried their rifles, bedrolls and saddlebags to the Dodge House.

The short, heavy-set woman behind the counter watched them enter the lobby. "Did you come-in with the wagon train?"

"Yes ma'am!" Bill answered. "And we're plumb tuckered out! Not to mention dirty as hell! And we want a room for a week . . . with a wide bed!"

Red watched him sign the register and pay for their quarters. The woman began talking again.

"Our restaurant is open from three in the morning, until eight at night! Seven days a week! The meals each cost one dollar, and you pay when you leave! I don't allow no loud noise or raising hell in the rooms!

And whores aren't permitted to come on the premises! Your room is 208 . . . upstairs at the end of the hall!" She handed the key to Bill.

Red followed him up a narrow stairway. One he had to ascend almost sideways, due to his wide shoulders and what he was carrying. The hallway was just as narrow.

"Here it is!" Bill said, upon arriving at door number 208. He unlocked the door and stepped into the room.

Red trailed him inside and closed the door. Then placed his saddlebags and bedroll on the floor near a lone window. The Winchester was laid on top of them.

He went to the window and looked out. And was staring down at the roof over another part of the hotel. Red checked the lock on the window. "No one can open it from the outside!" Then he went to the bed and pushed down on the mattress. "It seems like a lifetime since I slept in a bed!"

"I don't plan on sleeping here tonight!" Bill said.

Red nodded his agreement. "Our landlady is a tough ole girl!"

"She is that! But the rooms are clean, our property is safe, and the food is good!" Then Bill continued. "Let's buy some new duds, and visit a bathhouse."

* * * *

They left the bathhouse looking and smelling like different men. Clean, and wearing new broadcloth trousers, shirts, socks, and short underwear. Bill and Red had dropped-in at Smith's & Edwards' Mercantile. Bought several complete outfits, carried them to the room, and then took care of their appearance. It was early evening by the time all of this was accomplished.

"Is there a bank in Dodge City," Red asked, as they walked toward the hotel and some food. He was thinking about the large number of Double-Eagles in his left front trouser pocket.

Bill shook his head. "Starlet's my bank! I can trust her!" And he continued. "Did your Ma stand-up to your Pa?"

Red ran his right index finger over his mustache. "I don't recall hearing anyone speak of her . . . except my Father!"

"This Starlet and Alice Chambers got into a fight one time! They slugged it out, until an acting Marshal stepped in! Come to think of it . . . none of the Madams get along!"

"I'm glad to hear a Lawman is here!"

"No . . . Red! You're wearing the law on your hip! Law Officers don't live too long in this town!"

* * * *

Starlet's place of business was housed in a two-story wood frame house. One with a high false front. And Red thought he'd just entered an ordinary home. The place even had a parlor room. Four seated, not too dressed women, watched them come inside.

"BILL!" One of them yelled, and rose to her feet. "You're back! I'll get Starlet!" She left the parlor by way of a curtained doorway.

Red removed his hat when his partner did. Then watched another woman come into the room. The sight of her almost rocked him to his boot-heels. She had deep red hair . . . she was tall . . . and was wearing a pink loose fitting long-skirt chemise. The woman first hugged Bill . . . then kissed him.

"You didn't find her! Did you?"

"No, Starlet! I had trouble locating someone who even remembered Elvie Stover!"

"That's too bad! You must have stayed away too long!" Then she spotted Red. "Who's your friend? He's good looking!"

"Starlet Dalton . . . meet Red Schieman!"

Red shook the hand Starlet offered. "It's my pleasure, ma'am! You have a nice place here!"

"Oh . . . we get along! Are you going to stay the night too? I'm going to lock Bill in my room!"

"I . . . yes ma'am!"

"Good! I'll turn you over to Helen! She's the one who informed me Bill had returned!" Then Starlet touched Red's hair. "Our hair is almost the same shade! Which parent did you get yours from?"

Red felt his stomach knot, and thought, "here it comes!" Then he answered her. "From my Mother!"

Starlet laughed and moved her hand. "My Pa was a stubborn Missouri farmer! He gave me part of that . . . and the red hair too!"

Bill's laugh of relief had Starlet looking at him with curious eyes. "Red and I are sidekicks!"

"You . . . have a partner! I remember hearing that you'd never start riding with one!"

"Red's special, and not one bit selfish!"

"He must be!" Starlet replied, and motioned for Helen to join them. "This beautiful hunk of he-man is called . . . Red Schieman! Be nice to him!"

* * * *

A noise at the door had Red drawing his Colt from the holster. He opened one eye and observed Bill coming into the room. He was dressed in his short underwear, barefoot, wearing his gunbelt, and the untied leather thongs were hanging below his knees.

"Bill," a sleepy Helen said, sitting up, "it's barely daylight! What the hell are you doing in here?"

"I came to see if you're taking care of Red!"

"He's being taken damn good care of! Now get out of my room!"

"Hold it a minute, Helen!" Red said, while looking at Bill's bowed legs. "I'll bet you can crawl between his knees and never touch them!" Then Red busted out laughing.

"Hush, honey! You'll wake the other customers up . . . and they'll be mad!"

"Hell . . . we don't care about them! They're so hung-over and worn out by now, that Bill can whip them by himself!"

Bill grinned. Walked to the side of the bed and scooted Helen closer to Red. Then lay beside her. "You look too damn comfortable!"

"Dammit, Bill! If someone catches me in bed with two men . . . it'll ruin my reputation!"

"Your reputation was shot all to hell a long time ago! Stop acting like a virgin!"

Red laughed at both of them, and got off the bed. Then pulled his new trousers on. "He wants me to get up, Helen! And I'm as hungry as a gaunted bear!"

Bill rose from the bed too. "Get dressed, and I'll meet you downstairs!"

Red watched him leave. Then finished dressing. He buckled his gunbelt on, tied the holster down, and placed a five-dollar gold piece on a wash-basin stand. He left the room too.

"I'm damn glad this Starlet isn't your Ma!" Bill said, when they were on the street.

"Me too! Or I'd have to insist that you marry her! But I knew before she mentioned Missouri!"

"What tipped you off?" Bill was grinning.

"When we touched hands! The feeling wasn't right!"

Bill shook his head as they arrived at a restaurant in a large tent. And led the way inside. To the end of one of several long tables. The seats consisted of benches that were the same length as the tables. Plates loaded with a thick buffalo steak, beans, biscuits and gravy, were in front of him before he spoke again. "That leaves Starlet Lawson!"

Red ran his eyes over the few men in the place. And decided the hunters had eaten long before daybreak. They'd want as much daylight as possible for the killing and skinning. Then Red nodded his head at Bill. "How do we meet her?"

"This is Thursday," Bill answered, "and the Leaning-S will most likely come in on Saturday for supplies! We can hit the outfit up for a job!"

"Hell . . . I'm no cowhand! They'll have to be told that!"

"Punchers' get paid by the month . . . thirty dollars and found! And the spread furnishes mounts!" Then Bill continued. "Buffalo hiders' get from one dollar and twenty-five cents to three dollars and fifty cents per skin! A white hide will bring the lucky hunter up to one thousand dollars! That's damn good money if you can stomach the killing! Which means . . . any kind of ranch help is hard to come by!"

Red pursed his lips while sopping his plate clean. Then ate his last piece of biscuit. "I'll go along with that! Let's do it!"

* * * *

Saturday morning was born under a cloudless Kansas sky. It was July the thirteenth, 1872, and two men dressed as cowhands were lounging in front of Smith's & Edwards' mercantile.

Red and Bill were watching approaching small trails of dust materialize into wagons and riders. Many of the wagons were bearing men, women and children. Ranchers coming to Dodge City for supplies, and to visit with friends and distant neighbors. The riders trailing with wagons were escorts. Riders unaccompanied by wagons were in town for a little fun.

The sun, growing hotter by the hour, was almost overhead when another wagon and riders appeared from the south. A woman, with a mass of red hair showing under a man's big hat, was mounted and trailing the wagon. As was a young boy, a girl, and a man. Another older boy was handling the two-horse team's lines.

"That's the Leaning-S!" Bill said, when he could see the brand on the horses' hips. "And I know the man with them! But he's not Jim Lawson!"

"Who is he?"

"Pike Fenton! He went to work for the outfit at the start of it, and is as straight as they come!"

The youngster in the wagon turned the team, and pulled them up in front of Bill and Red. Bill went to meet the woman. And led her mount to the hitching-rail.

"I'm Bill Compton, Missus Lawson! Is Jim coming in?"

The question almost brought tears to her eyes, and she glanced at Pike Fenton.

"Bill doesn't know about Jim, Starlet! He's been away on a trip!"

"We lost Jim five months ago, Mister Compton!" Starlet answered. "He was shot in the Occident Saloon! I'm running the ranch!"

"My partner and I . . . Red Schieman, don't cotton to hide hunting! We're looking for work!"

"Well . . . we need hands!" She looked at Pike again.

"Bill Compton is a friend of mine, and as good a cowman as can be found! He has my recommendation!"

Starlet Lawson nodded her head, and looked at Red.

"I'm not a cowhand, ma'am! But I can ride, shoot, and I'm honest!"

"That's good enough for me, Red! When can you and Bill go to work?"

"Right Now! Our personals are at the Dodge House!"

"How about horses?"

"He has two . . . and I have one! They're at the stable!"

"Then go after them! You're both hired! There'll be room in the wagon for your bedrolls!" And Starlet continued. "Let me introduce you to my right hands! This is Pike Fenton! And the young man in the wagon is my son . . . James; my daughter here is called . . . Kerrie; and this redhead is . . . Tubar!"

Red had his hat off too, and nodded his head at each one. But when she introduced the youngest boy, he had an awful time keeping his face straight. This Starlet was his Mother . . . and she'd just introduced him to two brothers and a sister. James and Kerrie were both light-haired.

"Well, Red!" Bill said quickly, and slapped him on the back. "You load whatever our boss is buying, and I'll get our property!"

"Go with Bill, Pike!" Starlet said and smiled. "Wash some of that trail dust down!" She watched the two old friends walk away, and dismounted. Then turned to Red. "Come along!"

Red followed Starlet into the store. With her three children trailing him. And he was soon helping James carry sacks of flour and food staples to the wagon. The last sack was a hundred pounds of dried beans. Red set it in the front section of the bed, and turned to find James staring at his Colt.

"Are you good with that pistol?" James asked.

Red nodded his head. "I'm as good as most!"

"I want to kill the man that shot my Pa!"

"How old are you, James?"

"I was fourteen last month!"

"God," Red thought, "and I'll be eighteen in October! Only four years separates us!" Then he spoke to James again. "Who shot your Father?"

"A man called . . . Lester Knowles!"

"What started it?"

"Pa caught him and his men shooting buffalo on our range! They stampeded our herd!"

"How many head of cattle do you have?" Red continued.

"About eight thousand . . . not counting this springs crop of calves!"

"Lester Knowles will be dead long before you get old enough to go into a saloon, James! Men like that don't live very long!" And Red kept talking. "But you can do me a favor!"

James grinned. "What can I do that you can't?"

"You know more about cattle than I do! I'm going to need help!"

"JAMES!" Kerrie yelled from the doorway, and stopped their talking. "Ma wants you!"

Red followed the boy back into the store. Where Missus Lawson began fitting him with shirts until she found the proper size. She placed three with clothing she was buying for Tubar and Kerrie. Then she turned to Red, "Do you and Bill need anything? I can deduct it from your first month's pay!"

"No ma'am! We did our buying a couple of days ago!"

"But you're still young enough to like rock candy." And she handed a small paper sack to Red.

"Yes ma'am! I doubt that I'll ever outgrow it." Red reached into the bag for a piece, and passed the bag on to James.

"Stop being so formal, Red! Call me Starlet . . . like every-one else does!"

Red nodded his head. Then eyed Tubar. "You have an odd first name! Who gave it to you?"

"Ma did! She says it's special!"

* * * *

The Leaning-S headquarters was near a small lake, located six miles south of Dodge City. The lake formed after a creek had been dammed. And the headquarters consisted of a good size wood and sod main house; a barn; springhouse; two corrals; and two outhouses. The bunkhouse, which was totally sodhouse, had six bunks in it. Meals were cooked by Starlet, and were eaten in the main house.

Red assisted James in unloading the wagon and carrying supplies to the kitchen. Then headed for the bunkhouse. To find that Bill had already selected one of three empty bunks for him. And he met two more punchers. Sandy Ellis and Jimmy Bowers.

Pike, whom he'd already been introduced to, was a small graying man who reminded Red of Tommy Bayes. And Sandy was about the age of Bill and Pike.

Jimmy Bowers looked to be around twenty-five years old. Dark skinned, black wavy hair, trimmed beard and mustache. He was as tall, and almost as heavy as Red. And Red immediately tagged him as a self-styled ladies man.

And Red straightened the mattress on his bunk, spread a gray blanket over it, and looked for a place to put his rifle.

"There's a rack on the wall above the head of your bunk!" Pike said, from across the room.

Red turned his head and nodded at Pike. Then placed the Winchester on the wooden rack. And swung back around and looked into the man's eyes. They were friendly and full of curiosity. "Damn!" Red thought, as he glanced at Bill. Who was ignoring him. "He told Pike about me!"

"How's the food here, Pike?" Bill asked.

"Damn good! Starlet's a good cook!"

"Does the cattle stray very far from the creek and lake?" Bill continued.

"They graze all along the creek! Our big job is keeping the buffalo herds away from them! Hank Sitler just lost a big bunch of cattle! The buffs came through . . . and several thousand head left with them!"

Bill paused for a moment. Then hit Pike with another question. "Have you branded this spring's calves?" He watched Pike nod his head. "What about rustlers?"

"I can't say we have a rustler problem, Bill!" Pike answered, with his eyes on Red.

Red had already sensed that the string of questions were designed to provide him information. And he ask a question. "Who, besides Starlet, gives orders around here?"

"Pike does!" Sandy answered, and was looking at Jimmy. "But not everyone listens to him!"

Six

The hands were in the kitchen and eating breakfast. This was just before daybreak. And eggs, gravy, buffalo steaks, and biscuits were disappearing rapidly. They were being served by Starlet and Kerrie.

Red glanced at Bill. Caught his eye, and nodded his approval of the food. Then looked at Pike. The man was busy eating, but still watching him.

Pike rose from his seat, when his plate was clean and the cup in front of him was empty of coffee. This was a signal that it was time to go to work. Bill, Jimmy, Sandy and Red followed him back to the bunkhouse. Pike proceeded to give them their work orders.

"Jimmy, you take Red and ride along the creek to where the settlers are building! We don't want to lose any more stock between those damn high narrow banks! Sandy and Bill will work upstream!" Then Tubar and James came in. "Who do you want to work with, James?"

"Send me with Red!"

Pike nodded his head. "Tubar will trail along with me! We all have jerky! Let's get at it!"

"Damn," Red said, "I don't have any meat!"

"Yes you do!" James said. "I have enough for both of us!"

Red, Jimmy and James went to the barn for their bridles. But Jimmy came out carrying a lariat. Red climbed through an opening in the corral railing-fence and whistled for Amigo. He watched the Bay move away from the remuda, and come to him. Then Red slipped the bar-bit into his mouth. Worked the bridle behind his ears, buckled it in place, and led the big horse to where the drawbars were let down. James was waiting there with his mount for the day.

Then it was Jimmy's turn. The cowhand was in the corral too. He formed a loop . . . and with wrist movement Red couldn't follow with his eyes, flipped the loop and watched it settle over a buckskin mare's head.

Red grinned at Jimmy, as he led the mare through the opening. "Just remember, dammit, that I can't do that!"

But when Red had smoothed the blanket on the Bay's back, and loaded the heavy saddle on him, a new lariat was tied to it.

The three punchers rode away from headquarters and began walking their horses along the bank of the creek. With Red finding that he'd been missing Amigo. He waited for Jimmy to take charge . . . to quicken the pace. But this didn't happen.

"Come on!" Red said to his companions. And urged Amigo into a ground-covering running-walk.

"He's not keeping up!" James exclaimed, after several minutes had passed.

Red glanced back at Jimmy. And saw that he was far behind. "Does he do this very often?"

"Too much of the time, and Pike gets on him about it!"

"What does Jimmy do?"

"He just laughs!"

Red was silent for several moments. While digesting what James was telling him. "Where does Pike find him at?"

"In the kitchen drinking coffee . . . most of the time!"

"And bothering your Mother?" Red glanced to his left, and saw that the youngster was nodding his head. "Why hasn't Pike fired him?"

"Ma won't let him! Jimmy almost killed a man in a fight! It happened last year!"

"Does your Mother want to keep Jimmy on the ranch?"

"No . . . and he wants her to make him foreman!"

The lowing of one of the cattle stopped their talking. James and Red followed the stream around the base of a hill. Then spotted a cow at the edge of the creek bank. It was high at this point, and the stream was narrow.

"Well," Red said, when he saw her calf in the water. "This is what Pike sent us out for! Let's get the poor little devil out of there!"

"We'd better work from the other side!" James suggested. "That damn cow is ready to fight!"

Red took a good look at two long . . . sharp pointed horns, and followed James upstream to a place the horses could be ridden across. They approached the calf from that side.

James dismounted, and walked to where he could look down at the little critter. "I don't think this calf is stuck in mud, Red! It can't climb the bank to its Ma, and she won't move! So why should it!"

Red climbed out of the saddle too, ground-reined Amigo, and joined James on the bank. "Can we make the cow go downstream?" He asked, and spotted Jimmy coming toward them.

"Not without making her mad, and she may go upstream! The calf can't turn around!"

"Are all cattle this dumb?"

James laughed. "It's smart enough to stay with its Ma! And she's sticking with her baby!"

Red stared at James for several seconds. Then looked at the cow again. She was so full of milk, her teats were leaking. Then he untied the holster and unbuckled his gunbelt. Red's boots and socks came off next. "Drop your loop around its neck and get ready to lead it down the creek! I'll help it along!"

"Just be sure to get my lariat off!"

Red walked a ways upstream. Then slid down the bank and into the water. The water was only up to his knees, and the footing was solid. James was right. If the cow had moved out of sight . . . her offspring would've walked out of here.

He eased up behind the calf and pushed on its rump. But the little devil wouldn't budge.

"Twist its tail!" James suggested from above.

Red wound the calf's tail first one way . . . then the other. And was soundly kicked in the right shin. "She just kicked the hell out of my leg! Drop a loop down here!"

The loop was lowered to where Red could reach it, and he slipped it over the calf's head. James took up the slack. Red began pushing. But the calf still wouldn't move.

"Hell," Red growled, and took the loop from around the critter's neck. He picked her up and started wading downstream. Until coming to a place in the bank the calf could climb.

"LOOKOUT, RED!" James yelled. "Here comes the cow!"

Red looked up and saw over eight hundred pounds of muscle, bone and horns coming at him. He quickly set the calf down, turned around, and ran like hell. The bigger critter chased him back into the narrow part of the stream, Before she was satisfied that her baby was safe.

Howls of laughter heralded Red's arrival on top of the bank. He grinned at James, who was fairly rolling on the ground. "I'm going to throw your young ass over this high bank! If you don't stop laughing at me!" Then Red looked for Jimmy. "Where the hell did he go to?"

The tone of Red's voice sobered James. "Jimmy rode back up the creek the moment you started down the bank!"

Red picked his socks and boots up. Then moved upstream again to a place where he could sit on the bank and rinse dirt off his feet. He dried them with a bandanna, and put the socks and boots back on.

"Here's your gunbelt!" James said, from behind him.

Red rose to his feet. Buckled the gunbelt around his waist and tied the holster down. And all the while, looking at blonde-headed James. While wondering if the day would come when he'd tell the boy they were brothers.

They climbed back into their saddles and continued riding the creek bank. The sun was straight above them, when a small herd of buffalo was spotted. The huge shaggy animals were grazing in their direction.

Red eased back on the reins and pulled-up. "Let's stampede them back down the creek!"

"They'll run right over the place Ma sold to those foreigners! She won't like that!"

"Some of the wagon train people bought land out here?"

James nodded his head. "Ma sold them a hundred acres and the big spring on it! They're farmers!"

Red removed his hat. And wiped sweat off his forehead with a bandanna. Then eased the hat back on. "Where do we drive the buffalo to?"

James pointed to his right. In a southwestern direction. "Let's push them out there! Then twist their tails!"

The two riders moved their mounts to the left of the herd. Which Red now estimated to be five hundred head. Then they approached the leaders, while swinging a short section of their lariats over their head. The buffalo turned away from the strange sound made by the lariats.

Red and James hazed them a good mile from the creek. Then stuck cold steel spurs to their horses. They charged the buffalo while firing rifles into the air. The buffalo broke into a lumbering run. To disappear over a rise in the ground.

"We're being watched!" James said, after they started back to the creek. And pointed downstream.

Red was looking at two people. Riding without saddles, and mounted on broad-backed conestoga draft horses. It was Ingrid and her brother . . . Rolv. Red headed in their direction. And when they were close . . . he shook his head. Warning Ingrid that something wasn't right.

"We meet again!" She said, with a puzzled look on her face.

Red shook hands with Rolv. Then introduced James. "James Lawson . . . meet Ingrid Johansen and her brother . . . Rolv!"

James grinned. "We met when they came to see Ma about the land!"

"Are we to be neighbors now?" Ingrid continued, when James had finished.

Red nodded his head. "Bill and I work for James' mother! You could say . . . James is my boss on this ride!"

Ingrid glanced at the boy when he laughed. Her eyes locked onto his face. Then Red's. And she spoke to Rolv, using words James and Red couldn't understand. Rolv reined his mount away from them. In the direction of the creek.

"Go with him, James!" Red instructed the boy. And turned to Ingrid when they were out of hearing range. "I need a big favor!"

"You helped us! We'll help you! That is the way of my people!"

"Don't call me Tubar when we meet! In fact, don't say the name to anyone!"

"There is trouble?"

Red shook his head. "No . . . it's just that . . . " And he stopped talking. The right words wouldn't come.

"James looks like you! His mother could be yours!" Ingrid paused for a moment. While studying the strong face in front of her. "What is she to you?" When her question went unanswered, she tried again. "I have met all of the Lawson family! And the redheaded boy named . . . Tubar! I did not reveal my thoughts!"

Red nodded his head. While realizing he would one day have to tell Starlet who he was . . . or ride away. "Starlet Lawson is my Mother! But she doesn't know who I am!"

"Starlet doesn't know!"

"No . . . she left my Father when I was two years old!"

"I will not pry into your personal life! What do you wish to be called?"

"Red Schieman . . . for awhile!"

"Tubar Lane is a much nicer name!" Ingrid said, and continued. "I will call you Red Schieman!" Then she smiled. "It will be difficult! But I will somehow explain this new name to my people!"

Red grinned, when realizing she refused to use the name. "I appreciate this!"

Ingrid smiled again. "How long ago did your Mother leave you?"

Red studied Ingrid's eyes. Then answered her. "Almost sixteen years ago!" The expression changed to one of shocked surprise.

* * * *

Red and his younger companion returned to headquarters early in the evening. Their arrival was accompanied by the distant booming of large caliber buffalo rifles. Hiders were busy plying their trade against the huge animals. And the buffalo was a commissary on-foot to the Indian.

Supper was over by the time James and Red were washed up. And they met the other hands coming out of the kitchen. Each noted Red's muddy trouser legs. Which was a common occurrence on the ranch. But the steady look he laid-on Jimmy was something to ponder on.

"Come on in, boys!" Starlet said to James and Red. "I saved some for you! You can eat with Kerrie and me!"

"I'm sorry we're late!" Red said. "Do you always feed men who miss mealtime?"

Starlet placed her hand on Red's right arm. "Leaning-S punchers don't go hungry!" Then she set a plate of food on the table. "Dig in!"

Red waited until she and Kerrie were seated before he started eating. And vaguely noted that James followed his example in good manners. Red was still experiencing the sensation of Starlet touching him. The feeling was right.

* * * *

Red's arrival near the bunkhouse had him eyeballing Bill and Sandy. Who were outside, and facing a closed door.

"What's going on in there?"

Bill glanced at his partner's face. What he expected to see was there. "Pike rode-in early! Jimmy was here!"

"How bad is it?"

"Damn bad!" Sandy answered. "Pike's going to run him off this time!"

Red nodded his head. Pushed the door all the way open, and went into the bunkhouse. Pike was on his feet. Jimmy was lying on his bunk.

"How long did he stick with you?" Pike asked, when Red showed-up.

Red's eyes were on Jimmy's, and he thought, "here it comes! Sooner than I wanted it to!" Then he answered Pike, "Until we found a calf in the creek! Jimmy cut-out, and the cow almost got me!"

"By hell, Jimmy!" Pike growled. "Pack your saddlebags, and I'll get the pay you have coming! I want you and your horse off this ranch before dark!"

"I'm going!" Jimmy said, and came off the bunk. Then started by Red. "But not before I get a big piece of your old ass!"

Red stuck his left boot out and tripped Jimmy. Then pushed Pike through the doorway. Red stopped . . . and was facing Jimmy.

"YOU SON OF A BITCH!" Jimmy yelled, and jumped to his feet. Then advanced on Red.

But Red backed away. Through the doorway and away from the bunkhouse, Then Jimmy came to him.

He let the man have the first swing. A hard haymaker, targeted to end the fight quickly, had Red ducking under it. Then he jabbed with his left. The big fist caught Jimmy flush in the mouth . . . and blood trickled into his beard.

Then the two men closed. Grunts from the efforts of their swings, and from being hit, had the occupants of the main house rushing outside, to witness Jimmy landing on his back. A sneak right uppercut had found its mark.

Red stood over the man, slowly moving his fists, and let him get to his feet. He watched Jimmy cock his right, figuring again to end the fight with one massive blow. Red braced himself.

But Jimmy suddenly lowered his head and butted Red in the chest. The force of the impact knocked both men off their feet. Jimmy rose to his knees when Red did, and caught him high on the left cheekbone with a right. Red was on his back this time. And his Colt was jarred out of the holster.

Both men rose to their feet, Then closed again. Jimmy raised his left boot and raked it along Red's shin. The one the calf kicked.

Red was holding Jimmy with his left arm . . . and pounded him in the gut. Until the man sagged. He stepped back and measured Jimmy. And dropped him with a brutal right. Then Red wiped his mouth with the back of his left hand. The hand came away smeared with blood.

And Jimmy, slowly sitting up, pulled a long-bladed skinning knife from the top of his right boot, Then rose to his feet, "Let's see how good you are with a knife!"

"THAT'S ENOUGH, JIMMY?" Starlet yelled, and she had both men looking at the Winchester she was holding. "I won't have any knife fighting on the Leaning-S!"

"Bring the money due Jimmy, Starlet!" Pike said. "There's no more fight in him!" Then he spoke to Sandy. "Put his things in a saddlebag, and get his horse!"

Bill picked Red's .44-40 up, wiped it clean of dirt, and dropped it into the holster. "Well," he commented, while looking at his face, "you have another black-eye! This makes three since I've known you!"

Red grinned, and spat-out blood. "And I only have two eyes!" Then he gingerly touched his face. "I need a damn bath too."

"We have a swimming hole behind that hill!" Kerrie said, and pointed down the creek . . . away from the lake. "We bath there all the time!"

"Yes . . . we do, young lady!" Starlet said. "But you're not going this time!" Then she turned to Tubar and James. "You boys show Red where it is! Then bring him to me! I'll be the doctor!"

* * * *

Sandy, Bill and Pike watched from their beds, as Red came into the bunkhouse. They remained silent, while he took his gun-belt off and hung it on a wall-peg.

"We need to talk!" Bill said, as Red was pulling his boots off. "And for a starter, I had to tell Pike and Sandy who you are! You look too damn much like the Lawsons . . . and these fellows started asking questions!"

"I'm listening! If you don't mind me not looking at you!"

"The four of us, with the help of the boys, can handle the cow end of ranching! Starlet is good with the books, and she and Kerrie do the cooking! Hell, Red! We can make this a top outfit!"

"You must be tired of travelling!"

Bill grinned at his partner. "This Starlet's cooking has taken the notion out of me!"

"What we want to know," Pike added, "is when are you going to tell her?"

"I don't have the answer to that!" Red replied. "I need to know something first . . . and it can only come from Starlet!" Then he continued, "But you're right as rain about people becoming curious! Ingrid knows that Starlet has a . . . Tubar! And she put two and two together!"

Bill laughed. "I was wondering when you'd learn she lives down the creek from here!"

Red managed a half-grin. "How much of this outfit does Starlet allow you to run, Pike?"

"She lets me call the shots on everything outside of the main house! But I'm not young enough to do what you did to Jimmy anymore! We want you to run things out here!"

"Hell . . . I don't know one thing about ranching! James had to tell me how to get that damn little cow out of the creek!"

"You'll learn fast!" Sandy said. "With the three of us advising you!"

"Sandy's right!" Bill added. "And Pike here will still be the foreman . . . so Starlet won't know about you! But you'll make the tough decisions, and be our War Chief when things get out of hand!"

"You three have it all figured out! Don't you?"

"Hell, Red!" Pike exclaimed. "Starlet needs you! Don't you like it here?"

Red thought of the question he'd been asking himself for years: "Why did his Mother leave him behind?" Then he answered Pike. "Ask me that again sometime in the future! But for now, I'll go along with what you fellows want to do!"

"Good!" Pike continued. "Tomorrow we start culling-out old bulls, steers, and barren cows! We have a cattle-drive coming up!"

Seven

Mounts were brought from the corral to the barn. Saddled, and then tethered to the corral fence. Packages of jerky, and canteens full of water were necessary items on a roundup. When the outfit didn't have a chuck wagon.

Red stood looking at a big strawberry roan mare that Sandy had saddled for him. And the puncher's words were still echoing in his ears. "She's a little frisky at times . . . but a blame good cowpony!"

He untied the half-rein from the rail. Led her away from the fence and climbed into the saddle. The roan humped her back and crow-hopped toward the lake. With Red thinking, "if this is all you've got . . . you're in trouble!"

"HEY!" James yelled. "WAIT FOR ME!"

Red pulled on the reins. The mare stopped pitching, came to a complete stop, then shook herself. "Does she have any more bad habits?" He asked James, when he arrived. Then the horse turned until her tail was pointed downwind, spread her back legs and began peeing. And once the mare stopped . . . she remained standing in that position.

"She's ready to go to work now!" James said, while laughing.

"Who does this nasty horse belong to?"

"Pa!" And James continued. "Come on! Pike said for us to start at the south boundary, and work back this way!"

Red squeezed the roan with his legs, and she fell-in beside James' gelding. "Do you know what an old bull looks like?"

"Do you know what a grown steer looks like?" James grinned, when Red nodded his head. "Then we'll do all right!"

Once the horses were warm, James began alternating the pace from a running-walk to a lope. Then back to a running-walk. And it was close to noon when they came to the last bunch of cattle in sight.

They started their search for old stock, with James cutting-out the ones Pike wanted brought in. Red's job was to keep them bunched and moving.

The round-up lasted from Tuesday morning through Thursday. And by dusk, fifteen hundred thirty-seven head of old stuff and steers were in a large holding corral.

"This went-off real smooth with Jimmy gone!" Sandy observed. As the six mounted punchers took a breather.

"And we'll be in Buffalo City by late tomorrow evening!" Bill added, and was thinking of Starlet Dalton. But wouldn't say so . . . because of James and Tubar being present."

"Will they stay in there?" A suspicious Red asked. His first lesson was that cows are totally unpredictable.

"Most of these critters have been in there more than once!" Pike answered.

And come Friday morning, a hazy Kansas sky was looking down at an empty corral. The long Texas gate had been opened, and the small herd once again had to be rounded-up.

This renewed task was being accomplished by five riders. With the sixth, Sandy, searching for the man or men that turned them out. His effort was fruitful. The tracks of the horse Jimmy Bowers rode away on, were also near the Texas gate . . . and fresh.

"Why that no-good bastard!" Pike growled, when Sandy reported his find. "That's a hanging crime where I came from!"

The cattle ill-fated enough to be part of the drive, were still in the vicinity. And Pike rode to find Red. Who was still working with James. Pike motioned for Red to meet him away from the boy.

"That damn Jimmy came back and turned them loose!" He said, when Red rode-up. "Sandy found his horse's tracks at the gate!"

"And there's no mistake?"

"Not a chance! Sandy's good at reading sign!"

"How serious is this, Pike?"

"The hanging kind! And everyone in Dodge City most likely knows by now that he did it!"

Red stared at the ground for a moment. "Then we go get him!"

"Now . . . or after we deliver the herd?"

"After you sell the cattle! And Starlet isn't to know about Jimmy until it's done!"

* * * *

It was late Saturday afternoon, July the twentieth, 1872, when the Leaning-S arrived at the corral owned by one Charlie Rath. Who established outposts for the buffalo hiders. It was said that Charlie, who believed in joining them . . . if you can't lick them, had married a Cheyenne squaw of the "Little Bear Tribe!" A woman with the romantic name of: Maker Of Roads, and once married to Kit Carson.

The herd, now numbering fourteen hundred fifty-two, was short eighty-five head. Pike felt this group consisted mainly of steers . . . that stuck their tails straight up, and headed downstream like a southbound blue-northern.

But he delivered a bunch of sleek, fat critters, and left Charlie's mercantile with a pocket full of gold money. And the residents of Dodge City were waiting to see what the Leaning-S was going to do about Jimmy Bowers,

The crew of six mounted their horses and rode in the direction of Front Street. With Red wondering what to do with James and Tubar, when they located Jimmy.

He pulled-up when they came to Smith's & Edwards' store. And spoke to Pike. "Come and get me . . . when you find him!" Then Red motioned for Tubar and James to remain with him. They watched Pike, Sandy and Bill ride-off.

Red neck-reined Amigo to the hitching-rail. Dismounted, looped a half-rein around the rail, and led his charges toward the entrance. He let Tubar go inside first, and spoke to a curious James. Who wasn't asking questions.

"You're old enough to know we can't allow Jimmy to get away with what he did! But Tubar isn't! And you'll have to keep him here while I'm gone!" And Red handed James a dollar. "Buy some candy, and save a little for your Mother and sister."

Red trailed James inside, and saw Ingrid with Tubar. The Johansens were in for supplies. And the woman was again looking at Red's face .. . at his latest black-eye.

The expression of shocked surprise in her eyes, was still strong in Red's mind as he joined them.

"Did you sell your cattle?"

"Yes . . . but someone turned them out Thursday night! We drove in a smaller herd!"

"Such an act is very bad in my country!"

"It's the same here!" Red replied, as James showed-up with a sack of rock candy. Red reached into the sack and came out with two pieces. And handed one to the woman. Then grinned, when James maneuvered his younger brother away from them.

"Do you know who released your herd?"

"Yes! He's being looked for now!"

Ingrid nodded her head, and glanced at the other women in her family. Who were occupied with buying clothing and provisions. "Will Starlet sell us seven milk cows?"

"Can you catch them . . . and the calves?" Red watched Ingrid nod her head. "Then do it, and I'll tell Pike he's selling them to you! He'll inform Starlet!" Red stopped talking when Sandy came into the store.

"We found Jimmy! He's in the Occident Saloon!"

Red tipped his hat to Ingrid, and followed Sandy out of the mercantile. The walk to the saloon was a short one. And the appearance of the Leaning-S crew, with Bill carrying a lariat in his left hand, silenced the place.

Bill walked to where Jimmy was sitting. At a table with five other stud poker players. And Bill pointed at him with the hand holding the lariat.

"This man turned the Leaning-S's herd out of the corral Thursday night! He used to work for us, and we know his horse's sign!" Having said that, Bill continued. "All right, Jimmy, which one do you want? This noose . . . or me!"

There was no denial of the charges leveled at him, and Jimmy stared at Bill out of puffy eyes. This had his companions moving away from the table. "I want that bastard!" Jimmy pointed at Red.

"He's already kicked your butt once! Now it's my turn!"

Jimmy rose to his feet and stepped away from the table. He flexed the fingers on his right hand.

But Bill was watching his eyes . . . and they changed. Bill drew his Colt, and pulled the hammer and trigger back at the same time. The heavy .44-4O jumped upward. Two loud booms rattled stacks of shot-glasses on the bar. One bullet struck the floor between the two men . . . and one knocked Jimmy onto his back. The heels of Jimmy's boots beat a drum-roll on the floor, as an enlarging red spot surrounded the hole in the center of his chest.

"If anyone helped Jimmy," Red said, and moved alongside Bill, "I'm here to accommodate him!"

Bill slowly ran his eyes over the large room. "We can leave, partner! Jimmy was alone when he turned our cattle out!"

Red and Bill backed up until they were at the doorway. Then passed Pike and Sandy. Who were standing at each side of the opening, and holding Winchesters.

"By God!" Pike exclaimed, when all four of them were outside. "That was slick, Bill! Is Red as fast?"

"If he isn't . . . he soon will be!"

Red eyed Bill's face for a moment. "I'm going to deliver the boys to their Mother! You hombres have earned a night in town!"

"You'll need to take this gold with you!" Pike said.

"If anyone gets our money . . . he'll have to run it down!"

Eight

Pike waited until after breakfast to inform Starlet that Jimmy was dead. After he had assigned the day's work. His sudden return to the main house surprised her. She watched Pike pour two cups full of hot coffee. And waited for him to speak.

The foreman sat at the table, and looked up at Starlet. "Sit with me! I have something to tell you!" He waited until she was seated, and continued. "Where's Kerrie and Tubar at?"

"Kerrie went for a swim right after we cleaned up in here, and I sent Tubar to get her! That girl would move to the creek if I'd let her!"

Pike sipped on the dark liquid in his cup, while keeping his eyes on Starlet's face. "Jimmy's dead! He's the one that turned the herd out!"

"Did he have to die, Pike?"

"Yes . . . or the Leaning-S men would've had to stay out of town! And what he did is a hanging crime!"

Starlet's first impulse was to feel sorry for Jimmy. Until she remembered how she felt toward her husband's killer. "Did you hang him?"

"No . . . Bill called Jimmy's hand! And it was a fair gun-fight!"

"Did Bill get hurt, Pike"

The foreman shook his head. "Jimmy was out-classed all the way! Then Red asked if any of the men in the Occident helped him! And invited them to pick-up where Jimmy left off!"

Starlet looked into her cup for a moment. As if there were a message in it. "You like Red and Bill . . . don't you?"

"I sure as hell do! And you know what I think about Bill! That Red is of the same cut of cloth!"

"What is Red to Bill? Are they related?"

"I don't think so, Starlet! That boy is as tough as boot leather, and Bill says he's special!"

"There is something about him, Pike! When I touched Red the other evening . . . I almost hugged him! It was like touching one of my . . . ."

Starlet stopped talking and listened for a moment. "I hear Tubar! Something's wrong!"

"MA!" Tubar yelled, as he came running into the kitchen. "I can't find Kerrie! She's gone!"

* * * *

Weasel Leftler grinned, as he whittled the piece of wood he was holding into a toothpick. A sliver he'd sliced off of one of the store's counters. "Old Edwards almost jumped out of his boots when he saw me get this!" Weasel was a little man, with a ferret face. And the smell arominating from him was something fierce.

"He damn sure don't like you!" Don Carter said, and continued. "How many times has he ordered you out of this store?"

Weasel turned and glanced back at the mercantile. "More than a dozen times . . . I reckon! But we got what we came after!" Then he looked at their pack-train. Consisting of three mules, two horses and five Indian ponies. The animals were loaded with supplies: Powder; lead; shells; food staples; and whiskey. And were being tended by two Arapaho Indians. Mashinka and his squaw . . . Fallen Woman. Who was properly named when she was a toddler. The three men shared her.

Most of the provisions and other paraphernalia were for Don's and Weasel's customers. They ran a small trading post. Located northwest of Dodge City.

"We damn sure don't have everything," Don added, who equalled his partner in stink and size. "We need a girl to replace that Cheyenne squaw! She killed herself!"

"I've been trying to come up with a way to grab one of these whores! But they're too well guarded! And our customers want a white skinned woman!"

Don scratched a long, ill-kept, brown beard. "Send Mashinka and Fallen Woman out again! I heard some fellows talking about a real pretty blonde-headed woman! She belongs to some foreigners!"

"A blonde . . . huh!" Weasel said, and grinned. "Which direction does she live in?"

Don pointed toward the south. "On the other side of Jim Lawson's place! And tell them not to get one of the Lawson women! That outfit just killed a man for messing with their cattle!"

The warm Sunday sun was setting before the pack-train headed west, and the two Indians rode south. Mashinka and his woman headed for the nearest arroyo that ran in the direction they wanted to ride in. And as Indians often do, keeping to the arroyo allowed then to pass unseen through the countryside.

A new sun was rising overhead when it found them watching the lodge of the Lawson family. They were not to take a woman from this place. And the Arapahos returned to an arroyo. Continuing their search for the woman with hair like the sun. It was but a short distance from the lodge, when a sound from the creek had Mashinka reining his pony in that direction. There, in the water, was a woman with hair like the sun.

Mashinka left Fallen Woman with the ponies. He ran downstream until he could cross unseen to the far side. And using stands of bushes, and low places in the terrain, he was able to cat-foot up to the unsuspecting White woman. A sharp pistol-barrel blow to the head, in a place that would not mar the woman's beauty, put her in the land of many visions.

Then the warrior swung the naked White woman over his left shoulder like she were a sack of flour. Picked up her clothing, and waded the creek to where Fallen Woman waited with the ponies.

Mashinka loaded her face-down onto his pony. Mounted, and ran his eyes over the ground he had walked on. Grunted his satisfaction that his sign was slight, and pointed his pony in a northwest direction. The warrior kept to trails made by many cattle. His ponies' sign would soon be gone, like smoke rising through the limbs of a small tree.

The sun was straight overhead when the White woman moved. She raised her head, and Mashinka roughly pushed it back down.

Then Kerrie realized she was naked . . . and screamed. While struggling to get off the pony.

Fallen Woman pulled-up. Dismounted, and grabbed a handful of Kerrie's blonde hair. She jerked Kerrie off the pony, and swinging her fist like a man, Fallen Woman knocked her down.

Then the Arapaho squaw stared at Kerrie's white skin with contempt. And untied a heavy strip of tanned buffalo hide from around her waist. She whipped Kerrie until the fight was gone.

"Put on clothes!" Fallen Woman commanded, and threw them at Kerrie. The squaw watched her dress, and continued. "Get on pony!"

Mashinka took the lead again, with Kerrie now mounted behind him. And after riding when darkness was upon the land, when the sun had disappeared as many times as fingers on one of his hands, he and Fallen Woman were hidden near the trading post. They would take the White woman to Weasel when darkness was again upon the land. When the White hunters were gone.

This Saturday night, July the twenty-seventh, 1872, was moonless, and dark as the inside of a buffalo's belly. And when the last customer had ridden away, Mashinka and Fallen Woman rode to the back of the trading post. To a barn and small corral. He remained to put their ponies in the corral, and the Arapaho squaw shoved Kerrie toward a closed door in the back of the trading post.

"SON OF A BITCH!" Don yelled, when Kerrie was forced through the doorway. "They got that blonde-headed woman, Weasel!"

"Bring her out here so I can see her!"

Don got behind Kerrie. Placed his hands on her shoulders, and steered her through another doorway to the front of the trading post. "Just look at this little girl!"

Weasel was nodding his head, as he inspected Kerrie. "Nice . . . nice . . . very nice! Honey, you're going to make ole Weasel one hell of a lot of money!" Then he unbuttoned the boy's shirt Kerrie was wearing. Pulled it from around her shoulders, and stared at the black and blue welts on her back. "WHY THE HELL DID YOU WHIP HER?" He yelled at Fallen Woman.

"She bad!"

"We can't let those damn hiders see her like this!" Weasel continued, while glaring at the squaw. "She'll get us killed!"

"She has to be hidden until those marks are gone!" Don added. "We can tie her hands and feet, and put her in the storeroom! And we don't let one damn customer get close to that room!"

Kerrie re-buttoned her shirt while she was being hobbled like a horse. Then her hands were tied behind her. Don carried her to the back and into the storeroom. He closed the door on his way out.

Then the twelve year old girl cried for the first time since her abduction. She was old enough to know what they wanted her for.

Kerrie stopped sobbing when she heard a moan, and the back door opening and closing.

Kerrie tried to find a more comfortable position, and lay on her left side. Just as she heard the Indian woman coming toward the storeroom. The woman came in and made certain she was still tied, and left. Kerrie was again left alone in the pitch dark room. Then she heard the squaw fall down.

"Find out what that bitch is doing back there, Don!" Weasel said.

"Hell . . . she fell over a bucket!" Don exclaimed, when he got to her. "Fallen Woman is out cold! Help me get her to a bed!"

"Where the hell is that damn Mashinka when we need him?"

Kerrie heard them carry the woman into another room. And heard them return.

"Check that girl," Weasel said, "and make certain she can't get loose!"

"I'll do that now!" Don replied. He came into the store-room and inspected Kerrie's bonds. Then he left, and was closing the door when Kerrie heard him moan. The door swung open again, and Don was being pushed back into the room.

* * * *

Pike glanced at Starlet, and saw that she had both hands over her mouth. "Tell me that you're joking, Tubar!"

The white-faced boy was shaking his head. "I looked for Kerrie! She's gone!"

The foreman ran to where his horse was ground-reined. Jerked his rifle from the boot, jacked a shell into the firing chamber, and fired into the air. He did this three times. Paused . . . and fired three more shots. Then swung into the saddle.

Pike sunk his spurs into the horse's flanks, and busted the cold animal out. He didn't have to look to see where Starlet was. Kerrie's mother would be running toward the swimming hole too.

He pulled his mount to a plunging stop, just away from the creek. Then Pike slowly ran his eyes over the area.

"SHE'S NOT HERE!" Starlet screamed, when she arrived.

Pike fired three more shots into the air. A signal to the crew that something was wrong at headquarters. Then he reloaded the Winchester, dismounted, and put his arms around Starlet.

"I see them coming, Pike!" Tubar said, "Sandy and Bill will get here first!"

Pike was still holding his rifle when they pulled-up on heavily lathered horses,

"What the hell is wrong?" Sandy asked, and jumped to the ground.

"Kerrie came out here by herself," Pike answered, "and Tubar couldn't locate her!"

"Has she wandered off before?" Bill asked, and watched Red and James draw closer.

"No . . . and my shots would've brought her running back!"

Starlet backed out of Pike's arms, "You've got to find her!"

"We'll find her!" Pike replied, and was looking at Red. Who had just arrived with James. "Kerrie has disappeared!"

"From here?" Red asked, and watched Pike nod his head. "Sandy," Red continued, "see what you can find!"

Bill waited until Sandy had moved away from them, then looked at Red. "I'll ride to town and find out whose been in for supplies!"

"Saddle that strawberry roan . . . and run her damn legs off!"

"I'll take Starlet back to the house!" Pike added, and led her away from the creek.

"How soon can Bill get back, James?" Red asked.

James glanced at the sun. It was above them. "Pa did it in four hours one time . . . and he didn't change horses!"

Red nodded his head. While watching Sandy search for sign, and thinking about The Sailor's Cove. And of the stories of men taken to ships against their will, and forced to work during long sea voyages. What awaited Kerrie turned him cold on the inside.

Sandy walked the terrain for two fruitless hours . . . and gave it up. "It has to be Indians!" He said upon returning. "Few White men could cover their tracks so well!"

Red pursed his lips. "Let's hope Bill comes up with a lead! Either way, I'm getting ready for a long ride, Sandy, and you're going with me!"

They returned to the barn. Where Red inspected Amigo's shoes, and Sandy checked over his best horse. A black gelding. Then they saddled-up, with bedrolls, slickers, and a small sack of feed-corn, tied on top of full saddlebags. And two canteens of water were hanging from each saddle horn.

The sun was between high-noon and the western horizon when Bill returned. He was astride a borrowed horse, and his arrival brought everyone to the bunkhouse.

"Weasel Leftler was in town for supplies yesterday!" Bill said to Pike. "I've been told he's not above stealing a woman!"

"What does he do?" Red asked.

"The bastard runs a small trading post somewhere in this country!"

"Did he have an Arapaho Indian with him?" Sandy asked.

"Two," Bill answered, "a buck and a squaw!"

"That damn Mashinka!" Sandy continued. "I never did like him!"

"Do you know where this trading post is?" Red asked Sandy.

"Hell yes! I was there a couple of times . . . when I scouted under General Sheridan!" And the scout kept talking. "Weasel's place is located about sixty miles northwest of here!"

"And," Bill added, while eyeing Red, "those Arapahos will have to ride at night! They can't be seen with a White woman!"

Red stood looking at Starlet for a moment. "We want to get there first, Sandy! Let's ride!"

And Starlet, was watching the two with disbelief, as they rode off. Then she turned to Pike. "He's just a boy! Why didn't you send an older man with Sandy?"

Pike put his arms around her again. "If Weasel has Kerrie, they'll bring her back! In the meantime, we'll start our own search! If we don't find her tonight or tomorrow . . . I'll inform the Army that she's missing!"

Starlet pushed Pike away from her. "I know you're going to do all that! But dammit, it's not what I'm talking about! You let that boy make his own decision . . . and tell Sandy what to do! I want to know why!"

Pike glanced at Bill. "Because Red is good at what has to be done!"

The woman stamped her right foot out of frustration. "Tell me why, Pike!"

This time he looked to Bill for help, and Bill nodded his head. "Red Schieman isn't his real name!"

"What are you trying to tell me?"

"His real name is Tubar Lane . . . and he's going after his sister!"

Pike caught Starlet as she sank to the ground. "Help me take her to the house, Bill!" Then he spoke to James. "Get three horses ready to ride!"

They carried Starlet to her bedroom. Where Pike wiped her face with a wet washcloth. Then she began crying. "It wasn't my doing . . . it wasn't my doing!"

Pike remained long enough to make certain Starlet wouldn't faint again. Then went into the kitchen. Where he joined Bill and two very puzzled boys. "Go to your mother!" He instructed the youngsters.

"I'll start a fire, and heat this pot of breakfast coffee," Bill said.

"Damn!" Pike exclaimed, as he sat down. "I've never had to do anything this tough in my whole life! She just wouldn't let up!"

Bill nodded his head. "Now that she knows . . . the next move is up to her!"

"You're right about that! I hope her story keeps Red here!"

"I wonder what she'll tell him!"

"The truth, Bill!" Starlet said, from the doorway. "I'm not losing my first-born again!" She had her arms around Tubar and James.

* * * *

Sandy took the lead and urged the Black into a running-walk. "We'll ride six hours, and rest the horses two hours!"

"You set the pace! Amigo can keep up!"

Then their mounts were warm. And Sandy touched his in the flanks with spurs. The horse began an easy lope. A gait it would hold until lather appeared on its chest. Then the Black would be slowed to a running-walk until cooling off.

But once darkness had arrived, Sandy pulled his mount down to a walk. And followed arroyos when he could. The slower pace was to prevent injuries. The horses would have to be their eyes. To see spiny cactus, boulders and other obstacles.

They were following a meandering arroyo when the scout pulled-up. Both riders dismounted, loosened the cinches, and used their hats to give the horses a half-ration of water. Then fed them corn by hand.

Red laughed. "Bill is dead-set against hand-feeding a horse."

"I feel the same way. But we don't have a choice!"

"When do you figure we'll get to Weasel's place?"

Sandy was quiet for several moments. "Some time late tomorrow night! And every night, that little bastard will have two people on the place he doesn't know about!"

They sat on the ground after the horses had finished the corn. When two hours had gone by, Red and Sandy gave their mounts more water, and tightened the cinches. Then rode on.

The following morning found them working their way through a loosely-grouped herd of buffalo. And the steady boom of large rifles was reaching them. Sandy knew the sounds well, and was telling Red which rifle was fired as the noise was heard. "Big Fifty" Sharps were being used the most.

Tuesday, July the twenty-third, ended, with the two determined riders drawing nearer to the trading post.

And, early Wednesday morning, Sandy and Red were on the crest of a high hill. Looking down on a large sodhouse, a small barn, and a corral. The trading post was situated on a saddle between two lower hills, and near a tributary running into the Arkansas River. The little stream was called . . . Leftler's Creek.

"Mashinka isn't here yet!" Sandy said, as he eyeballed the surrounding countryside. "We'll spot him long before he arrives!" And he continued. "You can have the others, Red! But that Arapaho is mine!"

The younger man shrugged his shoulders. "Get some sleep! I'll keep watch!"

They were on the hill each coming day, and behind the trading post every night. Waiting for the Indians to show-up. Sandy and Red heard the hiders come and go. They had no quarrel with them.

Then it was Saturday night. Business at the trading post was as usual. Hiders came for whiskey, poker, and a woman. The lack of the latter, caused momentary spurts of ill-will between them and the management. But Weasel's promise of a pretty White woman calmed the situations.

Sandy and Red listened as a last customer rode away. The place was quiet again. With only two men inside. Weasel, and Don . . . his partner.

Both Red and Sandy heard the approaching ponies. And watched

the Arapahos pull-up at the corral. Then saw a squaw push Kerrie to the
trading post . . . and inside.

"SON OF A BITCH!" A man yelled. "They got that blonde headed
woman, Weasel!"

"Bring her out here so I can see her!"

Several minutes passed, with Sandy and Red keeping an eye on
Mashinka. And the lowered voices inside the trading post couldn't be
understood.

"WHY THE HELL DID YOU WHIP HER?"

The loud words reached Red and Sandy just as Mashinka left the
corral. Sandy cat-footed toward the door, and lay on the ground. The
unsuspecting brave walked past him. Only a low death-moan was heard
when Sandy drove his long bowie knife deep between the Indian's
shoulder blades.

Then Red eased to the door . . . opened it and stepped inside. This
part of the large sodhouse was almost dark, with a curtained doorway
separating him, the two White men, and the squaw.

The big man was moving toward another closed door when he heard
footsteps coming his way. Red backed against the wall, held his breath,
and watched the Arapaho woman open the closed door. Then she
entered the room.

Red moved his feet, and felt his right boot touch something. He
reached down, and came up holding a heavy wooden bucket. When the
squaw came out of the room . . . he knocked her down with one hard
swing to the head. Then put her left foot inside the bucket.

"Find out what that bitch is doing back there, Don!"

"Hell . . . she fell over a bucket!" Don exclaimed, when he got to
her. "Fallen Woman is out cold! Help me get her to a bed!"

Weasel came through the doorway, And reached for Fallen Woman's
arms. "Where the hell is that damn Mashinka when we need him!"

Red watched the two men carry the squaw into a room behind him,
and come back. They were so preoccupied with their thoughts, his near
presence wasn't sensed.

"Check that girl," Weasel said, "and make certain she can't get
loose!"

"I'll do that now!" Don replied. He opened the door and went into
the room.

Red was waiting for him when he returned. Don was closing the door, and walked into Red's left hand and the blade of a skinning knife. The big hand was over his mouth . . . the blade was buried in the pit of his stomach. Red pulled up on the knife. He lifted Don off his feet, and carried him back into the room. Closed the door, and withdrew the blade. Then wiped it clean on the dead man's trousers.

"Kerrie!" Red whispered, as he re-sheathed the knife.

"Is that you, Red?" A low voice said.

Red felt his way to the girl. He slowly worked the leather knots loose and untied her feet. Next he freed her hands. Then Kerrie was hugging him.

"Will you stay here until I get back?"

"Please don't make me, Red!"

"Then keep behind me!"

Red felt along the floor of the pitch-dark room until finding Don's left leg. He moved his hands up to his waist. Located Don's gunbelt, and pulled a pistol from its holster. Then pressed it into Kerrie's hands.

"Follow me . . . and don't make any noise!"

Red drew his Colt and opened the door. Listened for a moment, and walked to the curtained doorway. Then stepped into the front of the trading post. Weasel was sitting at a table, and had his back to him.

"Is the girl all right?"

"She's fine now!"

The strange voice had Weasel jumping to his feet and turning around. Red pulled the trigger. The Colt bucked in his hand, and the heavy bullet knocked Weasel back onto the table. Where he died.

Red went to the little man. And pulled a new Colt .44-4O from his holster. Then several loud clicks sent a cold shiver up Red's spine. He'd forgotten about the squaw. Her first shot missed him. Red brought both pistols up as he pivoted on his right foot, but the Arapaho woman wasn't doing the shooting.

Kerrie was holding a big Colt pistol with both hands. Her first shot had slammed the armed squaw against the wall. Then she shot her two more times.

"My God! But I'm sorry you had to do that!"

"Don't be, Red!" Young Kerrie replied, with tears in her eyes. "She whipped me hard!"

"We don't want to be found here if any of her people show up!" Sandy said, as he came from back of the sodhouse.

"Did you see what happened?" Red asked, and took the Colt Kerrie was holding.

"I saw it," Sandy answered, and hugged the girl. "She saved your life!"

Red grinned, and looked the place over. "Do you think the inside of this sodhouse will burn?"

Sandy eyeballed the bottles of whiskey behind a small bar, "I'll bet it will . . . and I've always wanted to put an end to Weasel Leftler's business!"

Nine

Sandy pulled-up about a mile away from the trading post. The flames inside the sodhouse were licking at the doors, and window framing. And were reflecting off surrounding hills.

"That fire will be seen for miles and miles!" He said, and pulled the Black around so he could look at Kerrie. Who was mounted on Weasel's bay mare. "You're going home to your Ma and brothers, honey!"

"That awful little man unbuttoned my shirt and looked at me, Sandy!"

"He won't ever look again! Red took care of that!"

"Red," Kerrie continued, "I heard Pa say when you saved a life . . . it became yours! If I were older, I'd keep you!"

"You wouldn't like my bad habits," and Red laughed. "But I'm glad you feel that way!"

"Well . . . staying here is a bad habit too!" Sandy added. "Let's move out!"

Sandy squeezed the Black with his legs and held him to a walk. He was in the lead again, and his direction was to the southeast. Kerrie was trailing the ex-scout, leading a pack mule, with Red following her.

He was holding a lead-rope in his left hand. Don's saddle horse was at the other end. And tied head to tail were three more horses, two mules and seven Indian ponies. Red was nigh-on to feeling like a horse-thief. But the Leaning-S's remuda was about to increase.

Sandy kept them in the saddle until a blue glow over the horizon in front of him, signalled the birth of a new day. He rode to the bottom of an arroyo and dismounted.

"We'll stay here for two hours and feed the horses!" He said.

"I hope you feed me!" Kerrie added, as she and Red got off their mounts. "They didn't give me anything to eat at the trading post!"

Red laughed, and handed her a package of jerky. "They will now!" Then he untied the feed-corn from behind his saddle. And gave each animal a handful until the sack was empty.

"They can make it to the Arkansas for water," Sandy said. "The railroad tracks run along this side of the river, and we'll follow them almost to Dodge City!"

"How far away are the tracks?" Red asked, and accepted the meat Kerrie was offering.

"We'll get there around noon!"

"I'll bet Ma is sick from worrying about me," Kerrie said, and started crying.

Red pulled the young girl into his arms. And stood holding Kerrie. . . letting her cry it out. He glanced at Sandy. The older man had tears in his eyes too.

"Come along, you two!" Sandy said, and wiped his eyes with a big red bandanna. "Let's get further away from that trading post!"

They rode-out, and within an hour were hearing buffalo rifles. In two more hours, the area around them was a beehive of activity. Slained buffalo dotted the land as far as they could see. With some men skinning-out the huge animals, and others loading green hides, and meat onto waiting wagons. Once loaded, drivers rushed the fresh meat and skins to Dodge City.

And at high noon, when the July sun was straight overhead, Sandy led them across the tracks and to the Arkansas River. Red rode Amigo into the river, and watered his string of critters all at the same time. When he arrived back at the tracks, a bunch of cavalrymen were with Sandy and Kerrie.

"This is Sergeant Barclay and his troopers, Red!" Sandy said. "They were looking for Kerrie too!"

Red nodded his head to the mounted Army men. "I'll buy drinks for all of you . . . if we can meet in one of the saloons!"

"And we'll take you up on that!" Sergeant Barclay replied. "But for now I have a report to make out! Fill me in on what happened!"

Red grinned at the Sergeant. "That's Sandy's chore! He knows how to talk to you people!"

"Weasel Leftler was in Dodge City the day before Kerrie disappeared . . . along with two Arapahos! The Indians' grabbed her!" And Sandy continued to the Sergeant. "Red and I trailed them to the trading post . . . and had to fight our way to Kerrie!"

"Will we find Weasel at the trading post?"

"Yep . . . but they're all dead! We had a hell of a shootout! And the damn place caught on fire during the ruckus! It was burning when we rode-out!"

Sergeant Barclay grinned, while eyeballing the pack mule, and the string of animals behind Red. "I've heard of you, Sandy Ellis! The report will be written your way!" Then the Cavalryman continued. "And we'll escort you back to town!"

* * * *

Three riders pulled-up on the crest of a rise in the terrain. And were looking across the creek at the Leaning-S's headquarters. Sandy reached for the pack-mule's lead-rope. And pointed to a woman who was running to meet them. "Go to her, Kerrie!"

Red watched Kerrie gallop her mount through the creek, and almost fall off the horse in her rush to reach Starlet. "That should be two happy females!"

"I'll be happy too . . . when I can get out of this saddle!"

The younger man grinned. Squeezed Amigo with his legs and headed for the barn. Where Pike and Bill were waiting for them.

"Well," Pike said, when they arrived, "you brought their remuda back! Did you turn Weasel and his bunch over to the Army?"

"We didn't leave anything for the cavalry! Red and I wiped the whole gang out!" Sandy answered, as they dismounted. He didn't mention Kerrie's part. "And you fellows can take care of our horses and mules!"

Bill grinned. "We were going to do that anyway! Starlet wants to see you!"

Sandy and Red walked to the main house. A tearful Starlet met them at the kitchen door.

"Come in, please! Both of you!"

Red and Sandy followed her inside. To find Kerrie, Tubar and James seated at the table. They waited for Starlet to speak.

Starlet hugged the older man. Then stepped back to wipe tears from her eyes. "How can I ever thank you enough, Sandy?"

"I've never had a daughter, Starlet! And bringing Kerrie home kind of made me feel like she was mine!"

Starlet nodded her understanding. "I won't insult you by offering money! What can I do for you?"

"You could try offering a cake!"

"I can handle that!" And she hugged Sandy again. "I'm going to keep Red here for awhile!"

Sandy left the kitchen and headed for the bunkhouse. Where Bill and Pike were again waiting. "You boys had better be nice to me! I get a cake out of this deal! I don't know what Red will end up with!"

"A mother!" Pike said. "I had to tell her!"

* * * *

And back at the main house, Red waited for Starlet to speak. He observed that James and Tubar were suddenly grinning at him. Kerrie looked confused.

Starlet reached out to touch Red with both hands, and drew them back. She did it a second time, and forced herself to put them behind her.

"I know your name isn't Red Schieman! Pike's letting you take over got me mad, and I raised so much hell . . . he told me!"

Red could only stare at her. "I . . . I wasn't ready to tell you who I am! The time wasn't right!"

"Would the right time have ever come?"

Red felt his mouth becoming dry. Words had to be said, that he didn't want to say. "I only know what Father told me!"

Starlet kept her eyes on Red's. "What did Raymond tell you?"

Her question made Red want to run. "That you ran-off when I was two years old! From where we lived in Wheeling!"

"What do you remember about me?"

"Just that you were tall and redheaded! And please . . . don't ask what Father said about you!"

"Your name is Tubar Gaylan Lane! And I have never . . . never been in Wheeling!"

Starlet 's words stunned Red into silence. And he already knew his middle name was Gaylan. "I wasn't born in Wheeling?"

"I had you in Boston, on October the ninth, 1854! Not in Wheeling!" Starlet continued, and was almost in tears again. "Please believe me, Tubar! I didn't leave you! Your Father took you from me!"

Red glanced at James. The boy motioned for him to go to Starlet . . . and that's all it took. The sobbing woman almost collapsed into his arms. Red helped her to one of the benches.

"You were my baby . . . and Raymond took you!" Starlet continued, gaining some control of herself. "I searched for you by myself! Then I met Jim Lawson and he helped me! Jim and I finally married! I had James, and we had to stop travelling! We went to so many towns! But Wheeling wasn't one of them!"

"Red is our brother!" Kerrie exclaimed, "And his name is Tubar too?"

"Yes, baby! This Tubar is part of our family . . . if he wants to be!"

"I need to know one thing! Why did Father take me from you?"

"My Mother, your Grandmother, became sick with the fever and was dying! I had to see her . . . and Raymond ordered me not to go! I couldn't take you because of the sickness!"

"And you went anyway!"

"Yes," Starlet replied. "Raymond left his job in a freighting office . . . and disappeared with you while I was away!"

Red thought of his Father, and how strict he was on him. And . . . he was the same way with his wife. Red kissed Starlet on the forehead and hugged her. "You're even with him now, Mother! A Chancellor bounced me out of school, and I left too!"

"We have a lot of catching up to do, son!"

"0 boy!" Tubar said. "You're staying!"

Red grinned at his youngest brother. While realizing he would always be known as . . . Red Lane. "This is my home too . . . and don't you dare call me Gaylan!"

"We'll somehow make room for you here in the house!"

Red shook his head. Then grinned. His Mother didn't want to call him by his new first name either. "Get use to it! I'm stuck with the name!" Then he continued. "I'll sleep in the bunkhouse!"

"Are you ready to take over the ranch?"

"No, Mother! Pike will be the foreman for awhile longer! We have that worked out!"

"I know that now!" And Starlet laughed.

"Are you going to call her Mother all the time?" Tubar asked.

"What's wrong with that?"

"It sounds sissyfied!"

Red laughed. "All right! I can call her Ma if you can! And I'll get out of here so you women can start on supper!"

"Tell the men it will be on time, Red!" Starlet said. "And take these boys with you!"

Red walked out of the main house and into a hot, cloudy, July day. It was late in the afternoon, a Tuesday, and the thirtieth day of the month. All of a sudden his world felt good.

"Things' must have turned out all right!" Bill commented from his bunk, as Red came through the doorway. With James and Tubar tailing him.

"They did!" Red replied. "And supper will be on time!"

"Did you get the straight of it?"

Red eyed his partner. "I sure as hell did! My Pa did the running! Plus I was born in Boston . . . not Wheeling! And my last name is Lane again!"

"Then you're officially our boss now!" Pike said.

"That's right," Red replied. "But we'll let you give most of the orders!" Then continued. "Did anything else happen while Sandy and I were gone?"

"Just the appearance of an occasional rider along the creek!"

Red went to his bunk and sat on it. "Is our cattle the reason?"

Pike shook his head. "It's that pretty blonde at the Johansen place! Several of the boys in town are trying to court her!"

"Red won't let that keep him awake nights!" Bill said, and busted out laughing.

* * * *

It was four days later, early on Saturday morning, when the Leaning-S wagon rolled away from headquarters. On its way to Dodge City for supplies. James was on the seat again and handling the lines.

And mounted on horses, were Starlet, Kerrie, Tubar, Red and Bill. Red was leading a saddled, but riderless bay mare. The one Kerrie rode away from the trading post. Which had fittingly been named Weasel.

The mare had been reshod by Bill. Its coat was curried, the tail and fetlocks trimmed, and the mane roached, Even the saddle and bridle were polished. The mare was a gift to Ingrid from Red. But would be presented by Starlet.

The small procession arrived in front of Smith's & Edwards' mercantile a little before noon. And James halted his team beside two much larger draft horses . . . harnessed to a big Conestoga wagon.

Red dismounted, and tethered Amigo and the mare to the rail. Then tied Starlet's horse next to his. The redheaded woman led the two youngest members of her brood into the store, Red, Bill and James remained outside.

"Helen's been wanting to see you!" Bill said, with his eyes on the other Starlet's place. It was on the far side of the tracks from where they were standing.

"Didn't you tell me these two woman don't like each other!"

Bill nodded his head. "Is that going to stop you from seeing Helen?"

"It just might! My Ma will get mad as hell if she gets wind of me going in there! Hell, Bill! She still thinks of me as a boy!" Red glanced at a grinning James. "I'll be able to get away with most things you do . . . but not that!"

Bill laughed. "Then I won't tell you where I'm going! Keep an eye on my horse and rifle!"

Red watched Bill walk away. And trailed James into the store. He ran his eyes over the place. Starlet and Kerrie were busy at a counter. Tubar was holding a sack that had to contain rock candy. The older Johansen women were in several locations, and Ingrid was in the company of a man. Whom Red had never seen. He kept his eyes on the couple until Ingrid spotted him. Red fully expected her to remain in the presence of the older man. This changed, when she formed the word "please" with her lips.

"James, bring me Tubar's sack of candy!"

The boy did as he was instructed. And once Red had the bag, he approached the blonde-headed woman and her friend.

"I'm sorry I'm late, Ingrid!" Red said, and handed her the sack. Then he offered his right hand to the stranger. "My name is Red Lane . . . and I appreciate you keeping her company for me!"

Ingrid smothered a laugh, as he walked away without shaking hands with Red. "Tom Parson will not be back to court me!"

Red didn't try to hide his laughing, as the upset man left the store. "Tom will . . . when he learns how old I am!" Then he reached into the sack and came out with two pieces of candy. Red put one in Ingrid's mouth . . . one in his, and continued. "Now that I've rescued you again, you can go about your business!"

Ingrid didn't move. But she did return the bag to him. "My age bothers you!"

"I was watching your eyes, Ingrid! They told me that I'm younger than you!"

"It is true! By almost two years! And I was surprised, but not upset by the difference!" And she kept talking. "You are a respected man! One who brought your sister back! I would be proud to have a man such as you, Red Lane!"

"Who the hell have you been talking to?" This only brought a smile, and Red continued. "Ma has a gift for you! It's tied to the hitching-rail out front! The saddle is a man's! And dress like the other women do when they ride the range! Wear boots, trousers, a shirt, and a man's hat!"

Ingrid's face lit-up . . . like a little girl about to receive her first doll. "You must not be here when this takes place! My parents have not met you! I would have to refuse the gift!"

Red nodded his understanding. Pitched the sack of candy to a waiting Tubar, and immediately left the store. To find Bill standing outside the doorway. "There's only one Starlet in there!"

"Hell . . . I haven't seen mine yet! I went into the Peacock Saloon for a drink, and ran into a Sergeant Barclay! It seems you owe half of Fort Dodge a drink!"

"Are they all there?"

"He says so, and those cavalry troopers are already licking their lips!"

"Then let's not keep the Army waiting! I have to get away from here anyway!"

They were crossing the tracks before Bill asked his question. "Are you running from that blonde?"

"In a sense! She can't accept the mare if I'm there! Her folks haven't met me!"

"But she can accept it from Starlet?"

"That's right!" Red answered, as they walked into the Peacock Saloon.

The building the Peacock was in . . . was about two hundred feet long. Freshly painted on the inside, and glittering as lights reflected off many large mirrors. And lined-up at a long dark-stained polished bar, were Sergeant Barclay and the troopers who escorted them almost to town.

Red shook hands with the Sergeant. Then spoke to a bartender who was standing-ready on the far side of the bar. "Serve these men what they want first! Then I'll have a beer!"

Sergeant Barclay made certain only the troopers on that patrol were waited-on. And he watched Red pay for the drinks. "Let's sit at a table!" He said to Bill and Red in a low voice. "I have some information for you!"

The Leaning-S hands trailed him to a table with little privacy. As this was a Saturday. Most of the tables were occupied by two kinds of customers: Men boozing on whiskey and beer . . . or men drinking and playing poker!

"You sound kind of serious!" Bill commented, when they were seated.

"I am, if the name . . . Lester Knowles, means anything to you!"

"He killed Jim Lawson!" Red replied, and paused for a moment. "I'm Starlet Lawson's son from an earlier marriage! But I never met Jim!"

"Jim Lawson was a good man!" The Sergeant continued. "Too good a man to be killed by that son of a bitch! Lester is fast with the Colt he packs, and mean as a mad copperhead! Plus he doesn't like foreigners! Especially the family your Ma sold land to!"

Bill grinned when Red's eyes got hard and bright. "Why is Knowles mad at the Johansens?"

Sergeant Barclay laughed. "That beautiful blonde won't have anything to do with him!"

"Has the bastard been bothering Ingrid Johansen?" Red asked.

"Is that her name?" Sergeant Barclay watched Red nod his head, then answered the question. "I won't say Lester's bothering her . . . because I only know of him approaching her two times! But one of my troopers heard him say that he was going to run a bunch of buffalo through their place!"

"Where did he hear this?" Red continued.

"In the Occident Saloon! Lester and his men are in there most every Saturday night!"

"How many men does Knowles have?" Bill asked, and watched the Sergeant hold five fingers up. "Do you think he'll go through with it?"

"I'll bet my stripes he does! And Lester has a stand west of your ranch! I sent a patrol out looking for it!"

"Damn!" Red exclaimed. "Stampeding our herd is the reason he and Jim got into it!"

"You ought to stick around, Red!" Bill said. "We'll pay Mister Knowles a visit tonight!"

Red shook his head. Killed his beer, and signalled for the bartender to bring another round. "I'd like to! But for now, I have to settle for hoping he doesn't do it!"

Ten

Red led Amigo out of the corral, and waited for James to slide the drawbars back into place. He had thought of asking Pike to send the boy out with Bill or Sandy. But whether the rider be man or boy, there was no controlling a wild stampede. Except to get the hell from in front of it. And let the critters run themselves out.

He led the Bay to the barn and ground-reined him. Then went inside for his gear. Red came back and placed the heavy Texas saddle on the ground . . . horned-end first. Then smoothed the blanket on the big horse's back. The saddle went-on next.

They rode due west from headquarters. As did four other riders: Pike and Tubar, Sandy and Bill. Their route led them across the creek, and toward the extreme western boundary of the ranch. The order from Pike was to start every head moving back to the creek . . . and beyond. Such was the seriousness of what Lester Knowles might do.

Red and James came to sleek cattle grazing on the short grass. Many were in bunches . . . some, mostly cows, their calves, and older bulls, were off by themselves. All were started in an eastern direction, and the riders hoped they kept moving.

The two young punchers worked to the south. And such was their haste to empty this part of the range of stock, they ate dried meat while in the saddle. The long hard hours of riding took them into the middle of a Monday evening. And the additional work forced upon the outfit was putting Red in a foul mood. One that boded ill-will toward a certain hide hunter.

Red pulled-up on the top of a high hill and surveyed the surrounding countryside. Then removed his hat, and wiped sweat off the headband with a bandanna.

"Tomorrow will be easier!" He commented to James. "All we have to do is stop them from drifting back!"

"I see buffalo south of here," James added. "But no cattle!"

Red nodded his agreement. "Where is the Johansen place?"

"Haven't you been there?"

"Nope . . . have you?"

The boy grinned. "We passed it a couple of hours ago!"

Red neck-reined Amigo around, while eyeing the boy. "Are you telling Ingrid what I do?"

"It could be one of several people!"

This made the older brother grin too. He squeezed the Bay with his legs and headed north. "Show me the Johansen outfit!"

They were on another hilltop. And evening had been replaced by early dusk. Red looked down at the small settlement. Five good sized sodhouses were being built at the same time. A big barn and corral were already finished, Shiny new wire marked the fence around a large garden-spot. With a Kansas setting sun reflecting off water ditched to the garden.

"Uh huh!" He exclaimed, and twisted in the saddle so he could see across a wide expanse of valley. It was to the west, "Let's have a look in this direction!"

He and James headed their mounts down the hillside and into the valley. This route took them to the creek and beyond. To the crest of another hill.

"That son of a bitch!" James exclaimed. "He's going to do it!"

Red stared with hardening eyes at six distant riders. And at what he figured to be a thousand head of buffalo. They were being drifted toward him and James, and would reach the settlement after dark.

"Get to the Johansens and tell them what's coming!" Red waited until the boy was at the foot of the hill. Then turned to face the slow-moving herd.

Red pulled the Winchester from the boot. And jacked a shell into the chamber. Then pushed another shell into the long magazine.

He stood the Bay . . . as the oncoming buffalo began making him nervous. And when the herd was within half a mile, the big horse was trying to break and run.

Red scolded his mount and put a short-rein on him. And eyed the middle two men, that were in a line behind the herd. He tied a knot in the reins and turned them loose. Then began firing at the two riders.

His first shot blew a man out of his saddle. Red squeezed off another shot at the second rider. But had to grab the reins with his left hand.

Amigo was trying to run again, and his Master was holding him back.

Red shoved the rifle back into the boot, just as Knowles and his men began firing their rifles . . . at him. The many leaded messengers of death hummed as they went by. With a plunging and rearing horse making him an elusive target. Then the leaders of the herd were running up the hillside.

The young foreman eased-up a little on the reins. Just enough to start Amigo down the safer side. His, was a rough plunging ride to the bottom. The horse wanted to run. His Master was still holding him back.

Several front-running buffalo were now at the top of the hill and spilling down the side in Red's direction. Red judged their speed, and putting Amigo's wide rump in front of a huge bull, he led the herd into the valley.

Red increased his mount's pace with the bull's. The herd had reached level ground. And when the buffalo were running full-out, Red began a wide swing to the right. And the bull was changing direction too.

Dust was spurting off the ground, as the hiders, who were now on top of the hill, began shooting long-range at Red. With him hoping that fast approaching darkness would mess-up their aim. That none of them got a lucky shot off.

Then Red spotted movement out of the corner of his left eye. He drew his Colt . . . and recognized Ingrid at the same time. The hard running mare was catching the slower galloping gelding.

"GO BACK!" He yelled, and knew he couldn't be heard. Then Ingrid was beside him.

Red looked to his left for the creek, and spotted the rows of trees that bordered it. And gave Amigo his head. He guided the Bay over a saddle between two hills. Then swung sharply to the right. The running buffalo continued straight ahead.

The gelding still had a lot of run in him. But the excitement of the stampede was gone. He began to slow when his Master eased back on the reins. Then the big horse was walking.

Red stared through dust and darkness at Ingrid. And refused to get mad at her . . . for riding into danger like that. But he did ask a simple question. "Why?"

"I wanted to help! The buffalo would have ruined all we have done!"

Red nodded his understanding, and rode closer to Ingrid. Then noticed her clothing. The woman was wearing spurred-boots, a man's trousers, a hat pulled down tightly on her head, and a man's shirt. He let his eyes linger on the shirt.

They walked their mounts until they had cooled off. And Red, after listening for Knowles outfit and not hearing it, rode into an arroyo. Then dismounted. He took the knot out of the reins, and ground-reined the gelding.

And when Red went to Ingrid, who was still mounted, the woman almost fell into his arms. Her weight carried them to the ground, and they rolled until he was on top.

Red could see Ingrid's lips. He waited until she moistened them, as a fire long-banked in him began to burn again, then kissed her. Their kiss was tender at first. And the fire flamed higher as the tip of Ingrid's searching tongue found his. Red moved to Ingrid's right.

He unbuttoned her shirt. Slipped his right hand inside and found a bare left breast. Ingrid arched her back while Red massaged the nipple. A low passionate moan was heard as the nipple hardened.

And a major battle was taking place inside Red. Between raw desire . . . and common sense. He pulled his hand away and out of her shirt. Then re-buttoned it.

"Why do you stop? I am willing!"

"I'm willing too . . . but a mistake will turn your folks against me!"

"Would you bed-me if I were a whore?"

"I haven't been bedding whores lately! And you're not a whore!"

Ingrid locked her arms around Red's neck. "No! But I am a woman in a hurry to become one with her man!"

* * * *

They rode away from the arroyo . . . with the drying lather on the horses showing. And beyond the two low hills where Red and Ingrid parted from the stampeding buffalo, they met James and the men in her family. Red pulled-up in front of her father,

"You should be proud of your daughter, sir! She helped me turn the buffalo!"

"That all you have to say?"

Red kept his eyes on Mister Johansen's face. "Well . . . she and her horse are safe! And your settlement!" Then he spoke to James. "Come on! We have a long ride in front of us!" He rode away from a father, and past a grinning brother.

"Boy!" James exclaimed, when they were away from the group. "He's mad! You and Ingrid stayed out here too long!"

Red laughed at his younger brother. "He didn't thank me for keeping the buffalo out of his damn garden either!"

It was nearing midnight when they arrived at headquarters. And part of a new moon had lighted their way. Pike, Sandy and Bill, met them at the barn. Then Starlet showed-up.

"You missed all the fun!" James said to them. "Lester Knowles kept his word!"

"Were any of the Johansens injured, Red?" Starlet asked.

"The buffalo didn't get to the settlement, Ma! Ingrid and I were able to lead them away!"

"That must have been some tricky riding!" Sandy commented.

"It was," James continued. "I watched part of it from on top of a hill! And Mister Johansen is mad at Red!"

"For helping them?"

"No, Ma! For keeping his daughter out there too long!"

The boys' Ma laughed. Then put her left hand on Red's arm. "Is it over with?"

Red shook his head. "I busted one of Knowles men with my rifle!"

"And we have to finish it!" Pike added to Starlet.

"Besides being mean, and slick with a pistol, what kind of a man is Knowles?"

"Cruel and vengeful, Red!" Sandy answered. "We'll need night-guards until Saturday!"

"Do you figure he'll try a stampede again?" Red continued.

"Nope . . . Lester will want to take care of you by himself! But his men will be closeby!"

"All right," Pike said, "We'll change our operation for a few days!" And he continued. "We can't work cattle . . . and leave this place unguarded! So we'll stay here! Guards will work four-hour night shifts! Starting right now, and Bill . . . You're on first!"

"We'll want to know for sure if Knowles is in town Saturday!" Red added. "Who do you want to send?"

"Hell," Pike said, "that's right! And the man will be Bill! Some of his friends know what's going on in Dodge City!"

"When do you want me to show-up there?" Bill asked, and was glad Starlet couldn't see his grin.

"Friday night! And if you're not back here by two o'clock the next afternoon . . . we're riding in!"

The short meeting in front of the barn ended with Pike's last words: "everybody sleep with their rifle!" And that's how the following five nights went. The four men shared guard duty at night . . . and a long gun was everyones' bedfellow.

Red spent the best part of the next morning, Tuesday's, cleaning-up a very dirty horse. This was done in the middle of the creek . . . when he could keep Amigo on his legs. The Bay had an affinity for laying in water. And amid howls of laughter from James, who was supposedly keeping watch, and efforts to get the critter up, Red managed to get the job done. Then had to tie the Bay up short, until he was completely dry. To keep him from rolling in the dirt.

Life on the Leaning-S was one of watchful waiting. The odd jobs that Pike could come up with, to keep the hands busy, were all finished by noon on Wednesday.

Saturday morning arrived with a sigh of relief. Headquarters, and the cattle in sight, were untouched, The long days were void of buffalo rifle shooting. As the hiders' were moving their stands with the herds.

But an underlying tenseness was in abundance. While wondering if Bill would return. And the time before two o'clock in the afternoon was well spent. Rifles and revolvers were cleaned, reloaded with fresh shells out of boxes, and blades were honed to a shaving-edge.

And at two o'clock, Red, Pike and Sandy, rode away from head-quarters alone. Starlet's oldest son had to tell her to stay behind.

* * * *

The atmosphere in Dodge City was one of high expectation. Residents from both sides of the tracks were mingling on this day. And there was much talk of an increase of residents in another place. It was Boot Hill, a final resting place for the unwanted. The graveyard, consisting of bodies, sand and buffalo grass, was located on a hill overlooking town. The "higher class of people" had a separate cemetery at the Fort.

Bill was seated in the shade of a store-front when he saw them coming. He dropped the stick he'd been whittling on, resheathed his bowie knife, and walked onto Front Street. The rest of the Leaning-S crew was riding into Dodge City from the west. It would put the August sun behind them.

"Where are they?" Pike asked, when they reached Bill.

"Inside the Occident!"

"Are we going to have to go in after Knowles?"

Bill shook his head. "The owner of the saloon doesn't want the place shot-up! And there won't be any rifles! The men living in town saw to that!"

"How many are with him?" Red asked.

"Five . . . and you killed Lester's baby brother!"

Red dismounted and led Amigo to the closest hitching-rail. Then tied a half-rein to it. He waited until his companions had tethered their horses. "Let's get it done!"

The four Leaning-S punchers lined up on Front Street. Between the railroad tracks and the false-front buildings. And began the short walk to the Occident Saloon. With an increasing crowd of people watching from the far side of the tracks.

"By God!" Sandy exclaimed, "Here they come!"

Five men had left the saloon. Walked to the center of the street. Faced to the west, and stood waiting.

"Which one is Knowles?"

"The big man in front of you, Red!" Bill answered. "The one with the blue shirt!" Bill held his left hand up. A signal that halted his outfit.

Lester Knowles had his eyes on Red. The cowhand that shot his brother. "I don't recall seeing you before the other day!" And he pointed at Red with his left hand.

But the younger man kept his eyes on Knowles'. "I'm Starlet Lawson's oldest son!"

"Where have you been?" The left hand moved again. In an effort to make Red watch it.

Red almost grinned. "In a school!"

Knowles motioned toward Red with the left hand. "Hell, you're nothing but a . . . " Then the hider's eyes changed.

Red's right hand came up. The Colt came with it. He pulled the hammer and trigger back at the same time. The .44-4O bucked, and Knowles was knocked to a sitting position. The tough hunter was struggling to raise a heavy revolver. And Red shot him again.

Front Street had exploded with gunfire. Red's left leg collapsed from under him. He was on his right knee and holding himself up with his left arm. And shot another hider that was sagging to the ground.

"Are you hit bad, Tubar?"

The street was suddenly quiet. And Red looked up when Bill spoke to him. The older man was almost doubled over. His left hand was covering a big hole in his chest. Blood was spurting between his fingers.

"BILL . . . NO!" Red yelled, as Bill stepped back in an attempt to keep his balance. Red dragged himself forward, trying to keep up. Then Bill was on his back.

"O GOD! You can't die on me!"

Bill touched Red's face. And his fingers came away wet. "Will you tell Starlet that I've always loved her?"

Red was crying. "I'll tell her!"

"And tell her she can have my . . . my . . . ."

"YOU BASTARDS!" Red screamed, and brought his Colt up. Only to have it taken away from him.

"They're all dead!" Sergeant Barclay's voice said. "Now let me tie something around that leg before we lose you!"

"Not my men too!" Red almost yelled the words.

"No dammit! The other two are only wounded . . . and not as serious as you are! Now keep still!"

"Take care of them first!"

"Doctor Tremaine is doing that now! He refused to get close to you!"

* * * *

Red, from on his Ma's bed, watched them lower Bill into a grave. But there were no more tears. He shut his eyes and laid his head back. Then thought of the shootout on Front Street. It seemed like a week ago . . . but had taken place yesterday.

He took a bullet in his left thigh . . . that missed the bone. Pike had a nasty tear along his right side . . . from an out of round bullet that had struck the ground first, Sandy had an ugly hole in his upper left arm. The bullet went in the front, and came out the back. He and Pike were the lucky ones. Bill was dead, and a big .44-4O piece of lead had to be cut out of Red's leg. This was done by the Army's doctor: Bill Tremaine.

Then the wounded men, and their horses, were taken to the Leaning-S. Their transportation was a rough-riding hired wagon. And Starlet was out of able punchers. Tubar and James dug the grave, while she and Kerrie prepared Bill for burial.

When this terrible task was completed, Starlet returned to the bedroom to see how her son was doing. Red had seemingly changed overnight. He rode out as a big serious minded boy. A man was brought home to her,

Red watched her come into the room. "James and Tubar will have to keep an eye on the herd, until Pike and Sandy can ride!"

She nodded her head, "Pike will be able to help them in two or three weeks! But I'm keeping Kerrie close to home!"

"You'll need to arm James with a revolver too! Does he know how to handle one?"

Starlet reluctantly nodded her head. "But I don't want him wearing a gunbelt to town! And Tubar only gets a rifle!"

"I have no argument with that!" And Red continued, while watching his Ma's face. "Bill told me that you and Starlet Dalton don't get along!"

Starlet Lawson frowned. Then laughed. "It's not something one of us did! For months people around here thought I was her, and she was me!"

Red tried to move his hurting leg to a more comfortable position. And managed a grin. "Bill left a message! I don't think she should have to wait a couple of months to get it!"

"I don't either, son!" Starlet Lawson was in deep thought for a moment. "I'll have to go to her! She's not allowed in the Dodge House!"

* * * *

It was the following morning, late, on Monday, August the twelfth, 1872, when Starlet Lawson entered Starlet Dalton's house. The sudden appearance of the redheaded woman stunned the girls who were seated in the parlor. Helen finally overcame her shock.

"Can I help you, Missus Lawson?"

"It's important that I see Starlet right away!"

"Yes ma'am!" Helen left the room, and returned to motion for the other girls to follow her. Once they were gone, Starlet Dalton entered the sitting room.

The two women, who greatly resembled one another, were silent for a moment. Starlet Lawson was the first to speak.

"Could we sit down?"

"Certainly, Missus Lawson! Please forgive my bad manners! It's just that I'm surprised to see you here!"

"Bill was able to talk some before he died!" Starlet Lawson continued. "His last thoughts were of you!"

Starlet Dalton began twisting a small handkerchief that she was holding. "Please tell me what he said!"

"Bill asked my son to tell you . . . that he always loved you! And what you were keeping for him is now yours!"

"Oh . . . why didn't he let me know about his feelings years ago!" Starlet Dalton exclaimed, while drying her eyes. "I only stayed in this business to be near him!"

"Some men are like that, Starlet!"

"I know only too well, Missus Lawson! How is Tubar?"

"He'll be fine in two or three months! You know, I have two sons named . . . Tubar! We have to call the oldest one . . . Red!"

"Is the youngest a redhead too?"

Starlet Lawson nodded her head, as she rose to her feet. "Bill is buried next to my husband! And you can come out anytime you want to!" She was getting ready to leave, when a small man came in.

"Which one of you Starlets has the last name of Lawson?" He asked, and removed his hat.

Starlet Dalton laughed. "She's Starlet Lawson!"

"My name is Tommy Bayes, ma'am! I'm looking for work!"

"I was just leaving, Mister Bayes! We can talk outside!"

"The Leaning-S is in need of a hand," Starlet continued, when they were on Front Street. "But my son should do hiring!"

"Is your son . . . Tubar Lane?"

The name stopped Starlet in her tracks. And the need to be cautious overcame her surprise. "Do you know him?"

"Yes ma'am! We came in on the same wagon train . . . from St. Louis to here! Tubar was with Bill Compton! They worked for the same Freighter I did!"

"What was your job?"

"Mule skinner, Missus Lawson! Bill's and Tubar's gear was in my prairie schooner! They slept in it too!" Tommy could see the indecision on Starlet's face, and continued. "I got real sick two-days west of here, and had to be taken to the Army hospital! Doctor Tremaine just let me go!"

"Then you know about the gunfight . . . and Bill!"

"Yes ma'am! Sergeant Barclay told me what happened! I'm real sorry that I wasn't here to side with them!"

"I have two sons named . . . Tubar, Tommy! We have to call the one you know . . . Red!" And Starlet had made a decision. "Do you own a horse?"

Tommy nodded his head. "I just bought me one and the gear I'll need!"

Eleven

The Corporal led his troopers north, away from a stream. And this was the second time Sergeant Barclay had assigned him this area to patrol. The first . . . when he located Lester Knowles' buffalo stand.

His chosen route took him from the creek, and to a large fenced-in garden. Corporal Heitman would ask for fresh water for his men's canteens. When his real purpose was to see a beautiful blonde-headed woman he'd heard about. By the name of Ingrid Johansen. And as he and twenty troopers approached several partially finished sodhouses . . . the small settlements residents stopped working to watch them ride-in.

Corporal Heitman pulled-up in front of the oldest man in the group. Then saluted him. "We need fresh water for our canteens, sir! With your permission, we'll fill them at the spring!"

"Sure! You can have water!"

The Cavalryman handed his canteen to the nearest trooper, and pointed toward a large flow of water bubbling from underground. Then ran his eyes over the place. "You people are doing a darn nice job!"

"We are carpenters and farmers!"

"How often do you go in for supplies?" Corporal Heitman continued, as he watched the woman called Ingrid come from behind one of the sodhouses.

The older man grinned. "When there is a need!"

This made the Corporal grin too. While thinking this must be her father, and other men have tried similar ruses. "Did you miss Saturday's gunfight? Six men died on Front Street!"

"We only know our neighbors!"

"They were in the shootout too! One of them was killed!"

"TUBAR!" Ingrid screamed, and started running toward the barn.

"ROLV!" Her father yelled. "HELP HER!"

"What's wrong?" Corporal Heitman continued.

"She cares for that one! Your news could be bad . . . very bad!"

The Corporal dismounted. And handed his reins to Ingrid's father.

"She can take my horse! I'll ride hers!" He watched Ingrid's father lead the Army mount to her. Then looked for his men. They were returning. And Ingrid was climbing onto his horse. "TROOPERS! ESCORT THAT WOMAN TO THE LAWSON PLACE!"

* * * *

The sound of running horses brought Red out of a restless sleep. He thought they were being attacked, and reached for his Colt.

Then Kerrie raced into the room. "Ingrid's riding in, and the Army's chasing her!"

"Hell . . . she must've heard one of us is dead, Kerrie! Tell her I'm in here!"

Kerrie ran out of the house to meet Ingrid. Who was just pulling up on a heavily lathered horse. "Red's in Ma's bedroom!"

Ingrid jumped to the ground and hot-footed it into the house. And didn't stop running until she was in the bedroom. "O my God! Your poor leg!" She dropped to her knees beside the bed, took Red's right hand in hers, and started crying.

Red withdrew the hand, and pulled her onto the bed with him. "I'm all right . . . I'm all right!"

"Who is dead?"

"Bill! We buried him yesterday!"

"And the others?"

"Pike and Sandy are both wounded! But they'll be up and around before I am!"

"Did you fight the men who tried to ruin our home?" Ingrid continued, and had stopped crying.

"Yes . . . and they won't trouble you again! Ever!"

Ingrid shook her head with sadness, "Poor Bill! He was a good friend to both of us!"

"Can I interrupt you?" Starlet asked from the doorway.

"Come on in, Ma!" Red answered.

Ingrid, red-faced, got off the bed and was hugged by Starlet. "Don't be embarrassed, honey!" The older woman said, and spoke to her son. "Have you decided what to do with Bill's property?"

"I'm going to keep the Gray and his guns!" And Red continued. "Does James have a rifle and pistol?"

"He has his Pa's!"

Red grinned at Ingrid. "Would your Pa let you keep a Colt revolver and Winchester rifle?"

"He will now . . . since he let me come to you!"

"Am I still in his doghouse?"

Ingrid laughed. "Yes . . . Father says you out-foxed him!"

"I hired a man while I was in town, Red!" Starlet said, breaking into their conversation.

"Is he here now?"

Starlet nodded her head. "I left him at the bunkhouse with Sandy and Pike! James likes him!"

"Kerrie said the Army chased you in here, Ingrid!" Red said, getting away from the man his Ma took-on.

"A Corporal loaned me his horse and an escort! But I out ran the troopers!"

"Are they still here?"

"No," Starlet answered. "They headed out as soon as the Corporal arrived on Ingrid's mare! But the Corporal told me to tell you that his last name is . . . Heitman!"

Red laughed. "I'm going to have to start carrying more money! Sergeant Barclay and his men almost broke me!" Then Red continued to his Ma. "And speaking of money . . . I have several hundred dollars in my right saddlebag! Ask James to bring it to you!" And Red paused, while thinking about Master Schieman at the Bramsley School for Boys. "But I have a use for some of it!"

"Are you taking more visitors, Yank?"

The familiar voice had Red staring at the doorway. "My God, Tommy! What the devil are you doing here?"

"I got sick a ways out of Dodge City and had to be brought back! But I'm fine now!"

Red grinned at his Ma. "You hired a damn good man!" Then he shook hands with Tommy. "Did Pike tell you that he was the foreman?"

"Nope! Pike said I'd get my orders from you!"

"Uh huh!" Red exclaimed. "And you met James!"

"Him and two other youngsters!"

"James knows all about this ranch! Ride with him . . . but you make the tough decisions!"

"I only had enough money for one horse, Red!"

"There's a good strawberry roan mare out there! Use her as part of your string! And one of those Indian ponies . . . if you want it!"

Then Red reached for Ingrid's left hand, and continued. "Do you remember this woman?"

"I sure do! I even met her!"

"There's a spare Colt in my bedroll! Give that to her, my Winchester, Bill's gunbelt and rifle boot! Then you and James deliver her home!"

"We'll be ready to ride when Ingrid is!"

Red watched Tommy leave, with Starlet trailing him. Then looked up at Ingrid. "I'll want to meet your folks before much longer!"

"I won't try to rush you!"

"Good girl! Now kiss me and go! My leg is hurting like hell!"

Twelve

Red came out of the barn and was carrying a bridle in his left hand. The first one he'd touched since the gunfight. And he looked upward at a wispy, cloudy Kansas sky.

This seventh of October, 1872, was the first Monday in the month. A cool steady wind was blowing from the northwest. One designed to push the buffalo south to warmer grazing. The rapidly disappearing herds would be followed by Comanche Indians . . . and the hiders. At the rate the huge animals were being gunned-down, the Indians would soon have to find another source of food. The kill during this year, and the next two years, was estimated to be in excess of three million head. Over a million buffalo had been slaughtered since the railroad arrived in Kansas.

Red tested his left leg again. The pain was gone and the big wound healed. Only a sunken, ugly scar was left to remind him of the shoot-out. Plus a dulling pain when he thought of Bill. Sandy and Pike had long been back in the saddle. Now it was time for him to return to work.

He walked past James and into the corral. Then whistled for Amigo. The Bay hadn't been ridden for weeks. But days' of being petted, while Red was getting well, brought the gelding to him. He slipped the bar-bit into Amigo's mouth, buckled the bridle into place, and led the big horse to where his saddle lay.

And James had one eye on what he was doing . . . and one on Red. "You've changed!"

Red eyeballed his younger brother from over the saddle, while pulling the cinch tight "We both lost a damn good friend! One like I wish my Pa had been! The difference is that I was there when it happened!"

The youngster nodded his understanding. And climbed into his saddle. "Tommy said he was going to get even with you!"

"What the hell for?" Red stuck his left boot in the stirrup and mounted the Bay. Then busted out laughing. He remembered giving Tommy the strawberry roan. "How does he like his new horse?"

James grinned. "Tommy thinks she's nasty too!"

"Come on!" Red said, and let his eyes linger on the big Colt pistol the boy was packing. "We have a lot of riding in front of us!"

They rode due east, straight as the crow flies, with Red's thoughts on the meeting he'd just had with his hands. The Leaning-S's new boss gave his first orders. Tubar would continue riding with Pike. Sandy and Tommy would work together! And one partner would have a branding iron tied behind his saddle. Unmarked calves would be branded where they found them.

But James and Red would be on the range for several days. A ride that would take them completely around the big spread. And this wasn't received too well by their Ma. James was a younger boy . . . fourteen years old, and he was his older brother's guide.

This was new country to Red, Part of the ranch he'd never ridden over. And keeping their mounts in a ground-covering running-walk, he studied the cattle they came to. The past summer's grazing had made them fat. But if what he'd been told about winter snows were true . . . the cattle would look much different come next spring.

Approaching dusk found them reining to the right and heading south. Then Red rode into a deep arroyo. He continued along the sandy bottom until coming to a long straight stretch, and pulled up in the middle of the area.

He dismounted, loosened the cinch, but left the saddle on. Then used his hat to give the Bay water.

James watched Red partial-out corn to his mount, "Aren't we going to unsaddle these horses?"

"Nope! Sandy told me several times not to undress them! We might have to get out of here in a damn hurry!"

That silenced the boy for several minutes. While taking care of his horse. "Do I get first watch?"

Red untied his bedroll from behind the saddle. Then led Amigo to the nearest bank. And nodded his head. "I'll take over at midnight! But neither one of us will get much sleep! We can't make a fire!"

Darkness brought cooler air. And each passing hour made it worse. James and Red, wrapped in their bedrolls, and holding their horses' reins, watched a sleepless night go by. Then, when the first rays of a new sun were above their camp, the cold became more severe.

They headed out of the arroyo and ate jerky as they rode. The warming rays of the sun were upon Red and James, as they came to the rim of another large arroyo. Both riders pulled-up at the same time.

"Jesus Christ!" James said, and felt his stomach churn.

Below them were three teamless loaded wagons. On the ground lay the bodies of seven hiders. All of them had been scalped.

Red pulled his rifle from the boot, and ran his eyes over the surrounding countryside without seeing movement. While wishing that he hadn't been eating. Then squeezed the Bay with his legs and rode into the arroyo.

"This must have happened sometime yesterday!" He said to James. "The blood isn't completely dry!"

"The Army will have to be told about this!" The youngster said from beside him.

Red looked the arroyo over. Then back at the bodies. Every hider had been downed with arrows. But two were more mutilated than the rest. Theirs were a terrible death . . . after the others had been scalped.

"They were chased into here, Red!" James exclaimed. "Look at the wheel marks on that bank!"

Red looked in the direction he was pointing in, while wondering how the wagons stayed upright. One was stacked high with green hides . . . two were loaded with near spoiling meat.

"Can you tell what kind of Indians did this?"

"No . . . and we won't find any of their dead either! Indians don't leave their kin laying around!"

Red climbed out of the saddle, and ground-reined the Bay away from the carnage. Then walked to the nearest hide hunter. The Indians' had taken the man's weapons and hat, which were also missing from his companions. And rode-off with their mules and horses.

Then he searched the hider for identification. Red was going through the pockets of the third hunter, when he found a letter from Gallipolis, Ohio. That, and two hundred thirty-one dollars, was all he could find on the seven. Only one cross would have a name on it: Gene Porter.

Red stood up and looked at James. Who was still mounted. "You'll have to help me bury them! See if you can find a place, and keep your eyes peeled for more Indians!"

"What kind of a place am I looking for?"

"Hell . . . I don't know! A wash-out in the bank, or a hole in the ground! Something like that!"

Red returned to where Amigo was standing and got back on him. Then watched James disappear around a bend in the arroyo. And the boy reappeared on a running horse. Red rode to meet him.

"I found the answer to our problem!" James said when they met. "Come on!"

The youngster stayed in the lead until they rounded the bend. Then dropped back beside his older brother, and pointed at six harnessed mules. Two were standing . . . and four were down. These were in a tangle of harness, trace chains and lines.

Red dismounted again, and walked around the mess of critters and gear. The harnesses on the wheel-team were still intact. "One of the hiders didn't want the Indians getting his mules! These were turned loose!"

"Why didn't he go with them?" James asked.

"He couldn't get on one . . . or wouldn't run-out on his buddies! But we'll damn sure take them with us!"

Red went to the Bay, and pushed his Winchester into the boot. Then led the gelding to James. "Don't just watch what I'm doing! You have to keep one eye looking for visitors!"

Then Red walked to the nearest standing mule. "Easy boy! Easy now!"

James laughed. "He's a girl!"

Red grinned. He unhooked one of the lead-mules, and led her to James. He cut the boy's lariat into six pieces for lead ropes. And tied one to the mule's bridle. "If we have to start running . . . turn this ugly devil loose!"

Then he approached the other lead-mule, and studied the nearest one on the ground. Red put his left hand over the downed mule's nostrils, so it could smell of him, and straddled its middle. While he unhooked the mule that was standing. Red took that one to James,

And he went back to eyeball the two swing-mules. They had to be unhooked next. "Oh boy! I hope these bastards have kicked themselves tired!"

"Pa said animals know when they're being helped!"

"I hope to hell your Pa is right!" Red said, and stepped among sixteen legs. With eight of them being kickers. He was moving slow, trying not to get the four mules excited.

Red unhooked both swing-mules from the wheel-team, and stepped away from them. Then reached for the swing-team's bridles. "Come on, dammit!" Red said, and began pulling. "You can get up!" But they didn't move.

"Some of those old mules are smart!" James said. "If they stand up . . . they have to work!" And he laughed. "We had a jenny that would lay down when she saw Pa coming!"

Red walked to Amigo and untied his unused lariat. And returned to the front mules. One hard swing of the coiled lariat had them scrambling up.

"We have a problem with one of the wheel-mules!" James said, as Red brought him two more to hold. "She has a broken front leg!"

Red returned to where they were lying. One of the remaining mule's right front leg was broken at the fetlock, "This is the reason they went down! And we'll have to shoot her!"

"Not until we get those hiders loaded! We want to be ready to ride when you do that!"

The older brother separated the two mules. And when the sound mule got up . . . the injured mule rose with it.

"They work side by side, Red!" James continued. "She won't be left behind!"

Red led the sound wheel-team mule to where James was waiting. Climbed onto Amigo, hung his lariat over the saddle horn, and reached for a lead-rope. He and two trailing critters headed back to the dead hiders.

"I'm glad these mules are used to smelling blood!" James commented when he arrived. "Or we'd have a hell of a bad time with them!"

Red dismounted, and tied his two lead-ropes to the saddle horn. Then pulled a pair of gloves on. And went to the closest dead man. He returned carrying the man as if he were a child, and placed him face-down over the back of the nearest mule.

James watched his big brother load five of them . . . and move two bodies forward. Onto the mules' withers. "Place those last two easy like!" He suggested. "Most mules don't like something back on their hips!"

Red hoisted the last hider onto the back of a mule. Two of the critters would be carrying a double load. Then he began cutting his lariat into pieces, and tying feet and hands together. Under the mules' bellies.

"How many do you want to lead?" He asked James, while inspecting his work.

"I can handle two of them!" James pointed at the animals with the heaviest loads. "But what about her?"

Red moved mules until James had the right ones. And tethered his three to the saddle horn. Then mounted Amigo, and tied a knot in his reins. "I sure as hell hate to do this!" Red said. Then drew his Colt . . . and shot the injured mule between the eyes.

They rode out of the arroyo. With Red looking up at the sun. He pointed the Bay in a west by north direction. "Which place is the closest? Ours . . . or the Johansens?"

"About the same!" James answered. "But we'd better head for home! Ma was a mite put-out over this ride!"

Red glanced at his brother. Who was riding to his right. "Why was that?"

James grinned. "Because tomorrow is your eighteenth birthday!"

"Oh hell!" Red exclaimed, as he thought of the date: October the ninth, 1872. "I forgot all about it!"

* * * *

A big bright moon, splashing light over the land, was high in the sky when Red and James arrived at headquarters. The sounds of many hoofs emptied the bunkhouse and main house. With Pike coming out of the shadows first.

"What the devil do you have loaded on those mules?"

"Dead hiders!" Red answered. "Indians trapped seven of them in a big arroyo sometime yesterday!"

"But where'd you get the mules? The Indians should've taken every team!"

"One of the hiders turned these loose, and a wheel-mule busted its front leg! The whole bunch was tangled-up! Four of them were down!"

"These poor . . . poor men!" Starlet said, as she walked along the string of mules. "Did you search them for names?"

"Yes, Ma!" Red continued. "Only one has a name! It's on a letter from Ohio! And we found over two hundred dollars on them! I have the letter and the money!"

"I'll return the letter to the writer," Starlet said. "With one of my own, and I'll send all of the money!"

Red watched Sandy ease an arrow out of a hider's back. Then go into the bunkhouse. "And I'll write a report for the Army!"

"Sell the mules!" His Ma continued. "I'll send that money too!"

"That can be done," Red replied, just as Sandy returned.

"This arrow belonged to a Comanche warrior!" Sandy said. "The Army will want to see it!"

Red nodded his head. Then glanced up at the moon. The night was like day. "We have a bunch of graves to dig! Let's get started on them now!"

"Happy birthday, son!" Starlet said, and hugged him. "But it won't seem like one!"

* * * *

It was late in the afternoon before the last grave was dug; the last sack-wrapped body was lowered; and the last grave was refilled with dirt. And Tommy drove a strong wooden cross into the ground at the head of one of the mounded graves. The name burned into the wood with a hot iron was: "Gene Porter!" The recipient of the letter.

And every man with the smell and feel of death on him, headed for the swimming hole. The slow moving creek water was cold. But this didn't stop young James from pulling his boots off. Then wading-in . . . clothing and all. It was but a short time before he had plenty of company.

Red returned to the bunkhouse bathed, and dressed in clean clothing. He buckled his gunbelt on and tied the holster down. Then stared at the two Comanche arrows Sandy had saved for the Army.

Then the oldest son headed for the main house. Red found his Ma at the kitchen table. Preparing a letter to someone called . . . Wanda Porter.

"I wonder if she's his wife . . . or daughter!" Red said, while looking over his Ma's shoulder.

Starlet had tears in her eyes when she glanced up. "I've been wondering the same thing!" Then she handed Red a sheet of writing paper, and a short, often used pencil. "Do the report for the Army! I need company at a time like this!"

Red tapped the top of the table a couple of times with the pencil, and began writing. He was signing his name to the report when James entered the kitchen.

"Several riders are coming-in!"

The older brother rose to his feet. Looked the report over, and followed James outside. Three strangers were standing their mounts in front of the bunkhouse. Pike was talking to one of them.

"This is my boss . . . Red Lane!" Pike said, when the oldest son joined them. "Tell it to him!"

Red shook hands with the stranger. Then waited for him to continue talking.

"I'm Earl Bates, and I represent the Wallace Cattle Company in Chicago! The owner . . . Russell Wallace, is in Dodge City, and he asks that you meet with him at seven o'clock this coming Saturday evening . . . in the Dodge House's restaurant! Hank Sitler will be there, and your neighbor to the west . . . Bob Haines! My next stop will be at Dakota Bailey's place!"

Red was having trouble keeping a friendly look on his face, because of the Wallace name. "What's the meeting about?"

"Mister Wallace wants to buy your cattle! That's all I'm at liberty to say! He wants to explain the deal personally! And," Earl continued, "he'll foot the bill for room and food!"

Red nodded his agreement. "Tell Mister Wallace the Leaning-S will be there!" Then Red continued, "You're welcome to eat with us!"

"I appreciate your offer," Earl replied. "But water for our horses will have to do! We still have a lot of country to cover!"

Red watched them ride-off, and turned to Pike. "How many ranches are close to us?"

"He just mentioned Bob Haines' Double-H-Slash, located to the west! Dakota Bailey's Rocking-B is east of us!"

"How large are their outfits?"

"About the size of ours! But Hank Sitler's spread is the biggest in Kansas!"

* * * *

A warming Saturday morning heralded the arrival of the Leaning-S on the south side of Dodge City. Starlet, Red, Sandy, and James in the wagon, rode past a huge corral that was being put-up by the railroad company. This was an item of high interest and curiosity.

Then they came to several curing houses . . . which produced buffalo hams. Meat that was destined for states located east of the Mississippi River. Buffalo tongues were being shipped in the same direction by the boxcar loads. And they rode past long, high piles of green hides. Permeating a strong stink that was an immediate cure for most newcomers appetites.

Red and Sandy, separated from Starlet and James, when they arrived on Front Street. And the two men pointed their horses east. In the direction of Fort Dodge. And Sandy, an ex-civilian Army scout, took Red straight to the headquarters building. The two arrows Sandy was holding, had Sergeant Barclay coming to meet them.

"Who did the Comanche get this time?" The Cavalryman asked, and reached for the arrows.

"Seven hiders!" Red answered. "James and I found them in an arroyo on the east side of the ranch! Here's a report I prepared for you!"

Sergeant Barclay read the document, while shaking his head. "And just one name in the whole bunch! I'll check around to see what outfit doesn't get back to town!" And he continued. "Are you here for the meeting at the Dodge House?"

Red nodded his head. "Sandy and I came to listen! Do you know something we don't?"

The Sergeant grinned. "Just that the buffalo will be gone in three or four years! And your cattle will be in greater demand by us and eastern buyers!"

Red glanced at Sandy. "And this Wallace outfit wants to put us in their pocket?"

"That's right!" Sergeant Barclay answered. "They'll want a set price, and a signed agreement!"

"We appreciate you telling us!" Red said, and turned to leave.

"There's one more thing," the Sergeant continued. "Lester Knowles came from a big family . . . and he has several brothers!"

"Are any of them in town?"

"I don't know, Red! But a new batch of gunslingers showed up three days ago!"

Sandy and Red left the long two-story building and mounted their horses. Then headed for town.

"Are you ready to wash some of this trail dust down."

Red nodded his head! "Let's board the horses first! Then see if it's safe for me to set foot in the Peacock!"

The Leaning-S punchers left horses, gear, and rifles at Cutler's & Wiley's blacksmith shop and stable. Then walked to the saloon. Red's pocket began feeling lighter the moment he entered the place. An Army Corporal was coming toward him.

"I'm Corporal Heitman, Mister Lane!"

Red shook the trooper's hand. "Do you know Sandy?"

"Yes sir!"

"I owe you a damn big drink! Are your men here!"

"Yes sir!"

"Then get them to the bar! The Leaning-S is buying!"

And as Sergeant Barclay did, Corporal Heitman made dead-certain only the troopers on the patrol were served. Red paid a bartender for the drinks. Then ordered a whiskey for Sandy and a beer for himself. He was paying for these, when a man's voice had him turning around.

"Are you Red Lane!"

Red watched Sandy grin, and relaxed. "Yes sir! But I don't know you!"

"I'm Dakota Bailey, son, and this is Bob Haines! We're neighbors of yours!"

Red shook hands with the older men. Dakota . . . a small slender man, with a wad of chewing tobacco behind his right cheek, and Bob . . . tall as the younger man looking at him. But not as heavy. "Can we buy you fellows a drink!"

"Hell yes!" Dakota answered, and continued. "We know you feed your hands gunpowder and boot-leather for supper! That was proved when you took-on Lester Knowles and his hiders! And we like Starlet Lawson! Now tell us where you stand on this meeting tonight!"

Red glanced at Sandy. "We haven't met any of the Wallaces yet! Earl Bates didn't tell us much either!"

"Well," Dakota continued, "they want to contract for our cattle . . . for the next five years!"

Red paused for a moment, as Bob Haines walked away from them. "I'll discuss this with Ma first! But I'm inclined to think other buyers will show-up too! That will drive the . . . ." Red stopped talking when someone touched his shoulder. It was Bob Haines. And Red turned to face him.

"This is Brad, Red! He's the son of Russell Wallace . . . the cattle buyer!"

Red ignored Brad's outstretched hand. And flattened him with one hard right punch. The younger Wallace pushed himself off the floor with his elbows. Then lowered his head back to the floor.

"RED!"

The tone of Sandy's voice was a warning. And Red took his eyes off Brad. To watch seven men leave the poker table they were sitting at. Red walked to the middle of the room.

"Son of a bitch!" Bob exclaimed. "You're sudden as hell!"

Red kept his eyes on the approaching strangers. Then watched them stop . . . and return to their table. He looked for the reason and found it. Sandy, Dakota and Bob were standing with him. Twenty troopers and one Corporal were behind him.

And Red laid his eyes on Brad Wallace again. Then laughed. Brad's left eye was closing faster . . . than Earl Bates could get him out of the saloon.

Bob Haines went to the bar for his drink, and came back grinning. "You ought to be ashamed of yourself, Red! Brad's out here on his honeymoon!"

Red thought of Elsa Stewart, and would've bet his last dollar that she was the bride. Then he motioned for Corporal Heitman and his men to belly-up to the bar again.

"Are you going to tell us what that was all about?" Sandy asked.

Red paid five dollars and twenty-five cents for the second time . . .

for twenty-one drinks. Then picked up his beer with his left hand. "Brad Wallace and I attended the same school in Baltimore, and we both liked the same girl! But Brad didn't play it straight!"

Sandy laughed, and glanced at the men who walked away from a certain gunfight. "I'd damn sure like to know what they're doing in Dodge City!"

"They're part of the Wallace outfit!" Red replied. Then he remembered what Bill said about the family. "Most of the Wallace men are ornery bastards!"

Thirteen

Sandy and Red left the Peacock in the company of Bob Haines and Dakota Bailey. The four cowmen walked to the far side of the railroad tracks. Then stopped to watch the entrance to the saloon.

"I was sure those hombres would tail us!" Dakota said.

"They would have, if the troopers weren't still in there!" Sandy added.

Then they went into the Dodge House. To find Starlet and James waiting near the doorway to the restaurant.

"The meeting could be delayed!" Starlet said. "Mister Wallace's son . . . Brad, was just helped to his room! He has an awful blackeye!"

Bob laughed. "The son ran into Red's big fist!"

"Red . . . you didn't!" Starlet exclaimed. And remembered what he'd said a Brad Wallace had done to him. Then she continued. "I met his wife!"

"Is her first name . . . Elsa?" Red asked, and grinned when his Ma nodded her head. "Brad didn't recognize me!"

"Ladies and gentlemen!" A woman's voice said, interrupting them. "The meeting will start in five minutes! Please come in, and find you a seat!"

Starlet led the way. And stopped beside the woman who made the announcement. "Elsa, this is my oldest son . . . Red Lane! I believe you know him as . . . Tubar!"

Red also stopped. Removed his hat and bowed. "It's nice seeing you again, Missus Wallace!" Then he followed his Ma into the restaurant.

Starlet went straight to a long table only three people were seated at. And sat beside the younger woman. Then they were joined by Red, Dakota, Sandy, James and Bob. Starlet made the introductions.

The people at the table were Ingrid Johansen and her parents. Who were also interested in what Russell Wallace had to say. And James, who was standing across the table from Ingrid, moved to allow Red to sit facing her.

Red leaned forward, so he could speak to his Ma in a low voice. "The Wallaces' want a five-year contract on our cattle!"

"How much are they willing to pay?"

"I don't know, Ma! But I'm suggesting we don't obligate the stock we sell to any buyer!"

Starlet nodded her agreement. Then looked past Red, at a man who had risen from his chair and was facing the people who were seated. The big room became quiet.

"I'm Bricen Mobley," the man said, "and Mister Wallace's business manager! It's my job to set the stage for him! And the first thing I want to cover is a market study we made on the buffalo!"

The Business Manager paused, while running his eyes over the ranchers and other interested people before him, and made eye contact with many of them. "Our study has determined that about four million head of buffalo roamed the plains before the killing began! Over a million have already been slaughtered . . . with a thirty percent harvest loss! I don't need to give you these numbers! The proof is out there! In the curing houses! The huge piles of hides, and the rail-car loads going east every day! The buffalo herds, as we see them now, are being wiped out! The hard fact is . . . the buffalo will be mostly gone by the end of 1874! Or into 1875!"

"This is the day of the buffalo . . . tomorrow will belong to cattle!" Bricen Mobley continued. "Yours, and from other sources! We foresee large herds coming here from as far away as Texas! This will naturally result in unstable prices! And it brings me to the owner of the Wallace Cattle Company! Ladies and gentlemen, Mister Russell Wallace!"

The introduction of the owner resulted in applause. It was started in the back of the room . . . by Earl Bates. Red, who was seated with his back to the front, was looking right at him.

So was Dakota. "This is nothing but a damn coyote trick!" He whispered to Red.

"Bricen has given you straight information!" Russell Wallace, a large florid-faced man, said. "Now I get to add to it! Our outfit has contracts with a number of packing companies! We have to meet our responsibilities . . . they must meet theirs! And all parties are in business to make money! Even the buffalo hunters! Whose operations will disappear with the herds!

And Russell Wallace continued. "How many of you have seen the big corral the railroad is building?" He watched every person in the restaurant raise one hand. "They're preparing for cattle herds! And the Wallace Cattle Company, run by my sons and me, is getting ready too! I won't beat around the bush about it, folks! We've spent a lot of money making preparations! The Wallace Cattle Company can afford the ups and downs of the cattle business! But . . . can you!"

The large man paused to let his words sink-in. "I'm here to offer you seven dollars and fifty cents for every head of cattle you bring-in! You'll receive this amount, regardless of the way prices go . . . guaranteed in writing! This is money you can bank on! And I need a five-year agreement to bank on! Think about it while we eat!"

"Do we still turn it down, Ma?" Red asked, as a thick buffalo steak was set in front of him.

"You're the man on our place," Starlet answered. "The decision is yours to make!"

Red nodded his head, and glanced toward the doorway. Brad and Elsa were there. With their eyes on him. Red studied Brad's swollen left eye, and grinned.

And Ingrid turned to look when Red grinned. With Elsa's eyes now on Ingrid . . . and Ingrid's eyes on Elsa. "Do you know her, Red?"

"I know both of them! They're Brad and Elsa Wallace! The ones I told you about!"

"Then they did marry!" Ingrid continued. "And you punched him in the eye?"

Red glanced at her Ma and Pa, who were looking at him. He nodded his head. "Brad had it coming!"

"Are you sorry he made trouble for you?" This had a father staring at his daughter.

"Me!" Red answered. "It was the best thing that could've happened!"

The meal was over, tables were being cleared, and Russell Wallace rose to face the room again. He was holding a sheet of paper in his right hand.

"Earl Bates, my Yard Manager, paid a visit to each rancher in the area!" The owner said. "Now it's time for us to bite the bullet . . . so to speak! Give me your decision as I call your brand!" Russell Wallace started with Hank Sitler's outfit . . . and was turned down. But he had better luck with the smaller spreads. With two out of three agreeing to a contract. Then he called the Bar-H-Slash.

Bob Haines rose to his feet. "I'll pass!"

"And The Rocking-B?"

"I'll go along with Bob!" Dakota answered.

"How about the Leaning-S?"

Red stood up. "We'll pass too!" And the three ranches south of Dodge City had turned the Wallace offer down.

Mister Wallace scanned the list, and nodded his head. Then continued. "I want to thank all of you for coming! And if those of you who want to go-it alone will kindly leave . . . the rest of us will discuss agreements!"

Red was rising to his feet when a waitress handed him a small piece of folded paper. He opened it, and frowned at a short message: "Please come to room 203 . . . Elsa" Then handed the note to his Ma.

"Is this her handwriting?" Starlet watched Red nod his head. "I don't like you going up there alone!"

Then Mister Johansen reached for the note, and he read it. "You go with Red!" He instructed his daughter.

Red and Ingrid left the restaurant and headed up the stairs to the second floor of the long building. The room was close to the stairway, and Red rapped on the door with the back of his left hand. To have it opened by Elsa.

"Please come in!" She said, and stepped aside to let Ingrid and Red into the bedroom.

Red walked to the center of the room and turned to face Elsa. "Ingrid Johansen . . . meet Elsa Stewart Wallace!"

The two women shook hands. Ingrid backed up until she came to the wall and remained standing there.

"Tell me why you hit Brad!" Elsa said to Red.

"I think you'd better ask him!"

"Dammit, Tubar, I did! And Brad said the same . . . ." Elsa stopped talking when Earl Bates and two other men came into the room. The last man to enter left the door open.

Earl was holding a Colt .44-40 in his right hand. And the barrel was pointed at Red's belt buckle. "What the hell are you doing in here with Missus Wallace?"

"I asked him to come, Earl!"

"Shut up, Elsa!" Earl said, and pulled the hammer back.

Red raised his hands to shoulder level. Then spoke to Elsa. "Brad set this up too! Just like he did when I got bounced out of school!" And Red was watching Earl's eyes. He didn't like what he saw. The man was in a killing mood.

Earl laughed. "We know how to take care of bastards that bother our women!"

"Tubar wasn't bothering me, Earl!"

"And . . . I said to shut up, Elsa!"

"What will you do with me?" Ingrid asked.

The realization that another woman was also in the room, had Earl's mouth dropping open. The Yard Manager lowered the Colt's hammer, and slid the pistol back into its holster.

Then Red hit Earl with a looping right haymaker. The hard blow, catching him over the left eye, knocked the man into the hallway.

"Touch that pistol and I will shoot you!"

Red watched one of Earl's companions move his left hand away from his holster. Then Red glanced at Ingrid and grinned. She was holding his revolver. And Red swung from the floor this time. He busted the man in the jaw. The force of this right punch propelled the gunman through a window, and to the ground far below. He landed between the Dodge House and Mueller's Boot Shop.

And Red turned around. "Where'd the last one go?"

Ingrid laughed. "He ran!" Then she eased the hammer down, and pitched the .44-40 to Red . . . butt first.

Red dropped the Colt into its holster. Then he and Ingrid cast accusing eyes on Elsa.

"Please believe me, Tubar!" Elsa said. "I didn't know this was planned! It was Brad's idea that I send the note to you!"

Red studied Elsa's face for a moment. "I believe you!" Then he and Ingrid left the room. Earl Bates was still lying in the hallway. Red pulled the Colt from his holster. And tossed it onto the bed in room 203.

"I don't know whether to go down first . . . or last!" Red said, when they came to the narrow stairway.

Ingrid laughed. "I will go first! You are a gentleman!" And when they arrived in the lobby, Starlet, James and Sandy were gone. Red looked inside the restaurant . . . even Ingrid's parents were missing. Then he and Ingrid walked out of the Dodge House. Into a cool October night. To find several people standing between the hotel and the boot shop.

"How'd you get my pistol?" Red asked, as they headed in that direction.

"I grabbed it when you hit Earl!"

Then James was with them. "Here are your coats! It's kind of cold out here!"

"What's going on!" The older brother asked, while watching James help Ingrid into her coat.

"A man fell out of an upstairs window! For awhile we thought he was dead!"

Ingrid laughed, as they joined the others. Dakota and Bob was also with them. "He didn't fall out of the window! Red knocked him through it!"

"What!" Mister Johansen almost yelled the word, and pointed at Red. "You did that with our daughter there?"

"I'm afraid so, sir! We walked into a trap!"

"Was Elsa in on it, Red?" Starlet asked.

"No, Ma! Brad suggested that she ask me to come up! Earl and two gunslingers came into the room while Elsa and I were talking! And Ingrid's being there saved my butt! Earl was set to shoot me . . . for bothering Elsa!"

"Where is he now?" Sandy asked.

"Earl was lying in the hallway when we left!" Ingrid almost laughed again. Her Father was staring at Red now. "And I threatened to shoot a man . . . if he touched his pistol!"

"Where did you get one?"

"I pulled it out of Red's holster, Father!"

"Well," Starlet said, "the supplies we came after are in the wagon! And the wagon is at the stable! Do we want to stay here tonight, Red?"

Red looked up at a disappearing moon. "I think we should head for home! Let the Wallaces' complete their contracts and catch a train back to Chicago!"

* * * *

The October days were getting shorter, cooler, and passing nights colder. And the Leaning-S people were sticking close to the ranch. The feeling between Red and Brad Wallace was nigh-on to bad, and Red had been a little rough on Earl Bates and one of his gunslingers.

And with the days sort of drifting peacefully by, work on the spread going well, the run-in with the Chicago-Wallaces was slowly being forgotten. Pike and Tubar were still riding partners. But Red had eased James into working alongside of Tommy Bayes. This put Sandy to trailing with his young boss.

It was ten-days after their night-ride out of Dodge City, when Red walked out of the bunkhouse to come face to face with Bob and Dakota. The foreman of the Leaning-S grinned at his new friends.

"You two can't be lost!" Red commented. Then watched Dakota unhook his canteen from the saddle horn and take a long drink of water. While wondering how he kept his chewing tobacco from going down with it.

Dakota capped the container and hung it back in place. Then wiped his mouth with the back of his right hand. "Are you having any trouble?"

Red shook his head. "Nope! We haven't been back in town, and you're the first company to show-up!"

"Bob and I have been in town checking with the other ranchers! And it appears only our outfits have been hit!"

Red saw that Sandy was approaching them from the barn, and was leading Amigo and his mount. "Water and feed these two horses, Sandy, and tie all four to the fence! Then come to the kitchen!" And Red looked up at Bob and Dakota. "Climb down! There was some coffee left over from breakfast!"

The three men caught Starlet and Kerrie cleaning-up. But their entrance stopped it. "Have you had breakfast?" Starlet asked.

"No, Missus Lawson," Bob answered, "and Dakota here is close to starving!"

"How does flapjacks, molasses, butter, eggs, and sweet milk sound?"

"Damn good!" Bob continued, "But where do you get the milk and butter from? Red's hands are too big for a cow's tit!"

Starlet laughed, stirred the coals in the stove, and added several sticks of wood. "This ranch has always had butter and milk! But I get it from the Johansens now!"

"Even in the summertime?" Dakota asked, as Sandy came in.

"Yes . . . we arrive at their place right before dark, and cover the containers with wet sacks!" Then Starlet spoke to Kerrie. "Pour the coffee!"

Red waited until their visitors were sipping hot coffee, before asking his question. "Are you going to tell me what brought you here? Besides Ma's cooking!"

"Bob and I have had a fire apiece since the Wallaces showed up!" Dakota answered. "Hell . . . we've never had a fire break-out before now!"

"Who the devil is doing it?"

"We don't know, Red! And some of our men can read sign almost as good as Sandy here!"

"Are the Wallaces gone?" Starlet asked.

"No ma'am!" Bob answered. "Brad and his wife are still at the Dodge House!"

Starlet set two plates of food on the table. Then poured two cups full of spring-house cool milk. "Did Earl Bates and his gunslingers leave?" She continued.

"Yep . . . on a train with the Old Man!"

"Where was the last fire?" Red asked.

"At my place!" Dakota answered, between bites, "I almost lost my damn barn!"

Red nodded his head. Then spoke to Sandy. "Ride over with Dakota . . . and have a look around!"

"Well," Bob said, with his mouth full of flapjack, "It's time for me to get home too! You fellows let me know what you find!"

* * * *

Dakota and Sandy rode-out directly after the two ranchers finished breakfast. With Sandy popping questions at Dakota in an effort to get all the information he could. But after a couple of hours there was only silence between them. Broken by the squeak of rubbing leather, and the jangle of bridle paraphernalia.

The ride to the Rocking-B's headquarters began in the middle of a Tuesday morning. And ended late Thursday afternoon. Sandy eyeballed a Kansas setting sun, put his horse in Dakota's corral, and began walking circles around the severely damaged barn. Each circle was larger than the one before it.

* * * *

Bob and Dakota arrived at the Leaning-S on Tuesday, October the twenty-second, 1872, and rode-off in separate directions on the same day. With Sandy trailing with Dakota.

Red watched them leave. Then untied the Bay from the corral fence, and headed south along the creek. Searching for cattle bogged-down between the few stretches of high banks, was a continuous task. Which was becoming more urgent since the water was getting colder each passing day.

It was shortly after noon, when Red found himself looking down at a large brindled-colored bull. The critter had waded between the banks until it came to belly-deep water, and there it stopped.

Red stepped out of the saddle, and knew he wasn't about to drop a loop over the big devil's head. He picked a large rock up and threw it at the bull. The animal moved forward one step, when the rock struck it on the back. This process, of one thrown rock . . . to one forward step, had Red ground-reining his horse, and following the bull to where it could get out of the creek. Then the bull decided the small walking cowboy had pestered it enough, and chased Red back to Amigo. The large animal lost interest in the game when its quarry merged with a bigger shape.

The lone rider retraced his route to headquarters. And the short day's ending had oil lamps burning in the main house and bunkhouse. Then they were extinguished, and a peaceful silence settled over their part of a cloudy world.

And sometime in the wee hours of the morning, a call by mother-nature awakened young Tubar and sent him scurrying in the direction of the outhouse. To find his way lighted by a burning barn.

"FIRE . . . FIRE!" Tubar yelled, and raced back to the house and his Ma. But a change of mind had him turning around and heading into the bunkhouse. "THE BARN'S ON FIRE, RED!"

"I heard you the first time!" Red said, and was pulling his trousers on. His boots went-on over bare feet. Then he followed Tubar out of the bunkhouse, and hot-footed it to the barn.

Flames were spreading up the back wall. And Red ran inside. To begin slinging saddles, blankets and other horse paraphernalia through the wide doorway. Then he was joined by Pike and Tommy. They emptied the building of everything but a stack of folded sacks. Those had already burned.

Red backed away as the heat became more intense. And watched helplessly while flames consumed the entire structure. Then the roof collapsed in a shower of glowing embers.

"This is no damn accident, Red!" Pike said. "The forge hasn't been used in a couple of weeks!"

Red went to his Ma. Who was watching her barn burn, with both hands over her mouth. And he put his arms around her. "With a little luck, we'll have a new barn before the first snow comes!"

"Your money will have to be used!"

"It's not my money, Ma! It's ours!"

Starlet began crying. Then she got mad. "What kind of a man would do this to us? He ought to be horsewhipped!"

"The son of a bitch will get worse than that . . . if I can find out who he is!" Red growled, and released his Ma. Then turned to his youngest brother. "How come you don't have a dog, Tubar?"

"A rattler bit my last dog in the head three times and it died! We haven't looked for another one!"

"Find you a pup the next time we ride to town!" Red continued, as Tubar grinned. Then Red looked toward the eastern horizon. Dawn was still a ways off.

"I think the Wallaces are behind these fires, Red!" Tommy said. "Rebuilding barns cost money . . . and a rancher sells cows to get money!"

Red stared at the ground for a moment. Then eyeballed the older man. "That has occurred to me too! But first we find the bastard who did this!" And Red kept talking to Tommy. "Use James and Tubar, and haul this mess away from here when it cools off!"

"What's my job in this?" Pike asked.

"Ride several wide circles around the place, and look for strange horse tracks! I'll search closer in on foot!"

"And I'll get breakfast started!" Starlet added. "This is going to be a long day!"

Daybreak dawned with Red watching Pike ride-off. On his way to look for sign. And Red began his walk around the completely burned barn . . . with his eyes searching the ground. As he had seen Sandy do.

The younger man, with an occasional look to see where Pike was, enlarged each new circle he walked. In an attempt to locate the route their late visitor had used.

By mid-morning Red was on the far side of the creek. Dogged in his determination to get a lead on the man. He entered the line of trees bordering the far side of the stream, while thinking about what Tommy said. That he felt the Wallace Cattle Company was behind the fires. And Red caught himself looking at an almost new store-bought . . . thrown horseshoe.

He picked the shoe up. Deciding that it could be re-used, and vaguely noted that a star had been stamped on the bottom. The Maker's trademark. And Red hung the piece of metal over the handle of his skinning knife.

Red widened his circle and continued searching. And by noon, as Bob and Dakota had done, he admitted his failure. The foreman was on his way to the kitchen, when he heard the rumble of wagon wheels.

Ingrid was mounted on her mare. Her mother and father were in one of the big wagons. Mister Johansen was handling the lines, and pulled-up beside Red.

"We saw the reflection of the fire on the clouds! Who burned your barn?" He asked.

"A late-night visitor, and he didn't leave his name!" Then Red continued. "Drive on to the house! Ma should have dinner ready."

The older man flicked the lines, and swung his two-horse team in the direction of the main house. Red led the mare to the corral fence. Where he tethered it. Then helped Ingrid dismount. He was wishing they were back in the arroyo, when her father joined them.

"I have extra lumber," Mister Johansen said, as he watched James and Tubar rake hot ashes to one side so they would cool. "You will have a better barn in ten days!"

Red grinned. "My men are good with cattle! But I don't know about working with wood!"

"My sons and I will do the work! But you will loan us Tubar!"

"We can pay for the lumber right-off," the younger man continued. "But something will have to be worked out on the labor!"

"You pay for what we use, Red! Our work will cost nothing!"

"Hell . . . I can't let you . . . ."

Mister Johansen stopped Red with an upraised right hand. "We will bring the lumber tomorrow!" He said, and walked away.

"You have helped us without pay!" Ingrid added. "Father will not allow you to pay him!"

Fourteen

It was a Monday, October the twenty-eighth, 1872, and Indian Summer was upon the land. The sunny morning was clear and windless, and four of the men from the Johansen family had moved into the bunkhouse. Missus Johansen and daughter Ingrid, were sleeping in the main house. A barn-raising was taking place on the Leaning-S.

And Tubar's part in all of this? He was the go-fer . . . going for all the small items they needed. And the framing for the new barn was near completion. It would even have a loft.

This is where Sandy found his foreman. Upon returning from the Rocking-B ranch. Red followed him to the corral.

"Son of a bitch!" Sandy exclaimed, as he stepped out of the saddle. "When did this one burn?"

"The night you rode-out! Tubar saw it first!"

Sandy stripped his gear off the horse. Then began rubbing it down with a sack he found hanging on the fence. "I didn't find a damn thing, Red! And I was almost crawling around on my hands and knees! Who did the looking here?"

"Pike and me! He came-up empty, and all I found was a thrown horseshoe that we can use again!"

Sandy watched the work on the barn for a moment. "I did run across the print of half of a store-bought shoe! But cattle had walked out the rest of the track!"

Red took his eyes off the barn, and looked at Sandy. "How do you know it was store-bought?"

"The blame thing had a star on it!"

"I'll be right back!" Red said, and went into the bunkhouse. He returned with the horseshoe. "I found this on the far side of the creek!"

Sandy reached for the shoe, and grinned when he saw the star. "This is the same design I saw at Dakota's place! It came off a big horse's front hoof, or a small horse!"

"How the devil can you tell that?"

"This is a double-ought size!"

"And we need to locate a large horse with this size matching front-shoe? One with the same star on it?"

"That's right, Red! The place to start is Cutler's Wiley's blacksmith shop! Let me saddle a fresh horse!"

The four-hours ride ended late in the afternoon. When Red and Sandy pulled-up in front of the blacksmith shop and ground reined their mounts. Then climbed out of the saddle.

Sandy looked the place over. And his eyes stopped on a youngster no older than Red. Who was shoveling manure away from the front of the shop. "I don't see either one of the owners, Red! Maybe Willie can help us!"

The older man reached for the horseshoe Red was holding, and walked up to Willie. With Red trailing him, "Have you shod a large horse during the past six days with a missing front shoe this size?"

Willie looked at the horseshoe in Sandy's hand. "A lot of big horses have small front feet!"

Sandy turned the horseshoe over. "How many wear shoes with this star on them?"

Willie shrugged his shoulders. "I don't pay any attention to markings!" And he turned to walk off. "I wish I could help you, Sandy! But I have to get something for Mister Wiley!"

He took two steps, before a big hand had him by the shirt collar. And Willie was looking into a pair of stony-blue eyes.

"Do you know who I am?" Red asked.

Willie nodded his head, while trying to get loose. "You're Red Lane! Starlet Lawson's son!"

Red tightened his grip on the collar. "Did you hear about the man that fell through an upstairs window at the Dodge House?" The Leaning-S foreman watched Willie nod his head again. "He didn't fall through that window . . . I knocked his ass through it!" And Red continued, "Someone burned my barn to the ground . . . and I'm upset over it! You tell Sandy what he wants to know, and be damn quick about it!"

"The horse is a big black gelding! It belongs to George Pippen! A whiskey drummer from St. Louis!"

"Is the horse here?" Red asked, and released Willie's collar,

"It's in a stall out back!"

"Take us to it!" Sandy said,

A subdued Willie led them through the shop and to several stalls. He stopped and pointed at one. Then watched Sandy go into the stall.

"This is the bastard's horse, Red!" The older man exclaimed, "The right-front shoe is the only one without a star on it!"

"What does Pippen look like?" Red asked Willie, as Sandy came out of the stall and closed the gate.

"He's about Sandy's size! George wears a brown coat and a black bowler hat all the time!"

"Even when he's out riding?" Sandy asked, and grinned when Willie nodded his head. "How long does his rides last?"

"Two or three days at a time! George told me he used to be a trapper, and likes being by himself!"

Red glanced at Sandy. Then ask Willie another question. "How much was Pippen going to pay you for that walk?"

Willie grinned, "Five dollars, and he's at the Occident playing poker!"

Red reached into his right-front trouser pocket and fished out a five-dollar gold piece. Then handed it to Willie, "Don't even think about leaving this place for at least an hour!"

Sandy and Red returned to their horses and climbed into the saddle. Then glanced at Willie to make certain he was staying put. And rode the short distance to the saloon.

"You stay close to the doorway when we get inside, Sandy!" Red said, and reached for the horseshoe with his left hand. Then he dismounted. Looped a half-rein around the hitching-rail, tugged on his Colt to make certain it was loose, and walked into the Occident.

Red ran his eyes along the bar. And was seeing hiders, local business men, saloon girls, and punchers. But no black bowler hat and brown coat.

Then he started at the nearest tables. Red moved forward, and worked his way toward the rear of the long room. At the midway point, he was headed in Pippen's direction like a bear going to a sweet-smelling honey tree.

"George Pippen!" Red said, and watched the man raise his head to look at him. "I have something that belongs to you!" Red scattered cards and money when he tossed the horseshoe onto the table.

Pippen picked the horseshoe up. Looked at the star and at the young redheaded man standing in front of him, "It's mine all right! Where'd you find it?"

"Across the creek from my barn . . . the one you burned down last Tuesday night!"

Red's words were a challenge, and they had the other players leaving their chairs. This end of the barroom became quiet. And the silence spread to the front like a fever.

Pippen rose to his feet. Removed the bowler hat, and with his right hand, picked up a bandanna that was lying on the table. He wiped perspiration from his forehead. "I'm not armed!" He said, and the hand disappeared behind the hat. That's when Red shot him in the chest. The force of the heavy .44-40 bullet slammed Pippen against the wall.

Red walked around the table and picked up the bowler hat. He holstered his Colt. Then reached into the hat and came out with a nickel-plated double-barrelled derringer. It was a .41 Remington. Red was holding the little pistol up for everyone to see . . . when another shot was heard.

"Does George Pippen have anymore amigos in here?" Sandy was heard to asked, in a loud voice.

Red looked the room over again, and shoved the little pistol deep into his left coat pocket. Then walked to where Pippen had been sitting. He turned the dead man's hole-card up, and saw that he had a club-flush working. And Red motioned for the other players to return to their seats.

"Somebody deal," Red said to them. "If he wins . . . I take the pot!" Red watched the cards land on the table. The dealer slid an eight of hearts in his direction.

But the Leaning-S's new barn was partially paid for when Red pocketed Pippen's playing money. The dead man's pockets were searched, and in addition to several more Double-Eagles, Red found himself staring at a key numbered 214. The same kind used by the Dodge House. He dropped a twenty dollar gold piece on the floor near Pippen, for burial money, and walked toward Sandy. Who was still at the saloon's front entrance.

"That son of a bitch wanted to shoot you in the back!" Sandy said, when Red reached him. And pointed at another dead man. This one had died in a sitting position . . . with his back against the bar.

The younger man looked at the body for a moment, then at Sandy. "I figure Pippen was the boss, partner! And I have the key to his room at the Dodge House! Let's go see what we can find! Then take our new black horse home!"

They backed out the doorway and to the hitching-rail. Untied their horses, and led them across the tracks. The horses were being tethered in front of the Dodge House, before Sandy spoke again.

"Who told you about that hat-trick?"

"Bill! He taught me everything I know!"

"Bill Compton wasn't his real name either, Red!" Sandy continued. "Bill was a loner when he showed up in Dodge City! A real curly-wolf! But Starlet Dalton took most of it out of him! And I was sure surprised when he came back with you!"

Red laughed. "Bill said he didn't usually saddle himself with a maverick!"

"You're damn sure no maverick now!" Sandy added, and kept talking as they entered the hotel. "Did you mean it . . . when you called me . . . partner? Or was it a slip of the tongue?"

Red was silent until they were in the upstairs hallway, and in front of room 214. "I meant it, Sandy! You and I work damn good together!" Then he unlocked the door and pushed it open.

An oil lamp, with a low flickering tongue of flame, was on a small table near the head of the bed. Red went inside first, and heard Sandy close the door. While he turned the wick up. The higher flame brightened the room.

He spotted a large valise on the floor, and picked it up. Then set it on the bed. And Red knelt down while looking under the bed. "Search every nook and cranny in here!" He said, and opened the valise.

"Here's his Winchester!" Sandy said, and placed it on the bed too.

Red glanced at the rifle, and reached into the bag. The first thing to come out was a frequently used gunbelt, with a holstered Colt .44-40. Then two full boxes of .44-40 shells, one of .41s, gun cleaning paraphernalia, and several items of clothing. Red was smelling of the trousers and shirts.

"None of these have a smoke-smell, Sandy!" Red said, and turned the valise upside-down. Then shook the remaining contents onto the bed. This consisted of toiletries and socks.

"Hell," Red continued. "There isn't one damn thing here to tie him to the Wallace outfit!"

"I haven't found anything either!" Sandy added. "But then I didn't expect to! Pippen was a professional!"

"Then let's take this bed apart!" Red returned everything to the bag, except the shells and gunbelt. These items and the rifle were placed on the floor.

Sandy helped him strip the covers off the bed. And they looked under the mattress. This search was fruitless too.

And a slight noise at the door, had both of them spinning around. To watch a folded piece of paper come sliding into the room. Red picked it up and walked closer to the lamp. Then unfolded it. A four-worded message said: "help is arriving tomorrow!"

Sandy drew his pistol. Walked to the door and opened it. Then stepped into the hallway and looked in both directions.

"There isn't a damn soul out here now, Red!"

"And this note was written by a man!" Red replied, from behind Sandy. While wishing he had seen Brad's handwriting. "Take this gunbelt, and let's get out of here!"

"Maybe Pippen's saddlebags will bring us better luck!" The older man said, when they came to the stairway.

Red let him go down first. Then glanced back along the hallway. No one was watching them. And he and Sandy had sacked Pippen's room without being discovered.

But Brad would learn tomorrow that his help was down by two men. Red was certain now that the Wallace Cattle Company was responsible for the fires. That Brad was left here to whip the small ranchers who refused to contract their cattle . . . into line.

The lobby was also empty when Red arrived at the foot of the stairs. And the aroma of cooking food from the restaurant, set his stomach to rumbling like an Indian war drum. But he trailed his new partner out to the hitching-rail.

Sandy and Red mounted their horses and rode back to the black-smith shop, A wet-moon showing above a distant horizon did little to light their way, But a lantern-carrying Willie did. He came out of the shop to meet them.

"Put Pippen's gear on that black gelding, Willie," Red said, "and bring him out here!"

"I figured you'd take him for part-payment on a new barn!" Willie replied. "He's saddled and ready to go!"

Red watched Willie return to the shop, and come back leading the Black. "Is everything still in the saddlebags!" He continued.

"It's all there! But I have to admit to wanting to open them!"

The Leaning-S foreman nodded his understanding. "Maybe I can do something more for you! Someone may come for this Black! It's worth another five-dollars to know the person's name!"

Willie grinned. "That's a fair deal! Do I tell who took George's pretty horse?"

"Yes . . . say that I came and demanded that you turn the Black over to me! And that's all, dammit! Don't tell anyone that you helped us!"

"Don't worry about me doing that, Red!" Willie replied. "My Ma didn't bring a fool into this world!" And he handed the gelding's reins to him.

Red pushed Pippen's Winchester into the boot on the Black's saddle, and squeezed the Bay with his legs. He and Sandy rode out of Dodge City. In the direction of the Leaning-S.

It was after midnight when they arrived at headquarters. Sandy and Red unsaddled the horses. Carried their gear toward the bunkhouse, and was met by a rifle-bearing Tommy Bayes.

"Did you get the bastard that burned our barn?"

"We sure as hell did!" Sandy answered. "And there's another saddle at the corral!"

"Then I'll lug it in for you!"

Red and Sandy entered the dark bunkhouse, and placed the saddles and other horse paraphernalia on the floor near the door. Then Red felt his way to a table in the center of the room, raked a match across the top of the table, and lit a lamp. He kept the flame low. So the people sleeping wouldn't be disturbed. But four pairs of eyes were watching him from bunks . . . and two pairs from bedrolls. They saw Sandy place an extra gunbelt on the table, and Tommy come in with a third saddle and rifle. The Winchester went on the table too.

"Is someone missing a horse?" Mister Johansen asked.

Red nodded his head. Then walked to where Pippen's saddle was laying, and untied the bags. "The man that destroyed our barn lost his life, and a real nice black gelding!" Then Red carried the saddlebags to his bunk.

Tommy watched Red open the right bag. "You ought to do that in the kitchen! Starlet's been up all night waiting for you and Sandy to get back!"

The foreman picked the saddlebags up and eyed Sandy, "Why don't you come too! Maybe she'll feed us!"

A lighted kitchen awaited their arrival. Red and Sandy entered the good smelling room to find coffee boiling, and two plates of warm food on the table. Plus Starlet, Ingrid, and her Ma were here.

Red dropped the saddlebags on the table in front of Ingrid. "See what you can find in these!" Then he pulled Pippen's derringer and the box of .41 shells from his coat pocket, and handed them to his Ma. "Here's a toy for you and something to shoot in it!"

"Isn't this a pretty thing!" Starlet exclaimed, "Do I get to try it out?"

"Sure you do!" Her son answered, and took his first bite of cooked food since yesterday morning. "But not in here!"

Then Red watched Ingrid remove an almost empty package of jerky from the left bag. It was all that side contained. And the blonde-headed woman dumped the contents of the right saddlebag onto the table.

Red shook his head. "You were right, Sandy! George Pippen wasn't about to lead us or anyone else to his employer!" The items on the table were ones any rider would own. And most were tools to take care of the Black.

Ingrid placed the dead man's property back in the right saddlebag. But left the jerky on the table. "Where was the man staying?" She asked,

"At the Dodge House!" Red answered. "And this was slipped under the door while we were in his room!" Red pulled the sheet of paper from a shirt pocket and slid it across the table to Ingrid. Who read it, and passed the short message to Starlet.

"What does this mean?" Starlet asked, and handed the paper to Missus Johansen.

"First," Sandy answered, "it means that George Pippen and the man who wrote the note didn't want to be seen together! Second . . . he'll know by morning that Red has his message! And lastly, setting fire to ranchers' barns isn't getting the job done! Red and I figure things will get a mite rougher when the help shows up!"

"Do the men know about this?" Starlet asked Red,

"No, Ma! But they will after breakfast!"

* * * *

Red watched his crew come back inside the bunkhouse. As they did every morning to get their day's work orders. And he was thinking about what took place when they left the kitchen.

James had rushed through his breakfast and left ahead of the rest of them. And when Ingrid's father came out, the boy was holding the reins to Pippen's black gelding. The horse was saddled, Pippen's rifle was in the boot, and his buckled gunbelt was hanging over the saddle horn.

Then James led the Black to Mister Johansen and handed him the reins. The surprised man turned to Red . . . who had followed him outside.

"Why did the boy do that?"

"The horse, and the outfit is a gift from us to you!" Red had answered. "But don't ride the gelding to town until I tell you it's safe to!" Then he walked away from the older man.

Red forced his mind back to the matter at hand . . . the Wallace Cattle Company. And he filled his men in on what took place last night. Then, trying not to embarrass any of them who couldn't read, the young foreman read the message to them.

"Sandy and I," Red continued, "both feel this has come to a shooting situation! The Leaning-S has become a damn big burr under Russell Wallace's saddle blanket! He wants to control our cattle before other buyers show-up! In addition, we've stung him pretty hard!"

"Why don't we ride to town and meet their train?" Pike asked,

Sandy laughed, as Mister Johansen and his sons came inside the bunkhouse. "Hell, Pike! We'd have to take-on six out of every ten men that got off! Killing buffalo is a fast money business, and some of the hiders are nothing but outlaws and renegades!"

"I don't know too much about this kind of fight we're facing," Red continued. "But Sandy does . . . and I'm for letting him tell us what to do! If any of you disagree . . . speak up now!" There was no dissenter, and Red sat down.

"Our best chance to survive an attack is right here!" Sandy said. "On our own ground! And we know they have to come after us! To make a damn big example of the Leaning-S!"

"When do you figure Wallace's men will hit us?" Red asked.

"One of them will be out there watching us by tomorrow night!" Sandy continued. "And that gives us ample time to get ready! We'll fight them the Indians' way!"

"We came here from Sweden!" Mister Johansen said, when Sandy stopped talking. "Our ancestors were warriors! And now we are Americans! We will fight with you!"

Sandy nodded his head, and grinned at Red. "Let's get a big surprise ready for the nervy bastards!"

* * * *

Red flexed the fingers on his big hands. In an effort to loosen them up. They were stiff and sore from yesterday's digging. And the long hole he was lying in was covered with several of Mister Johansen's thick boards. Sacks covered the boards, and a deep pile of dirt was over them. Clumps of grass and small cactus, had been planted in the dirt. From a short distance, the mound of fresh dirt appeared to be part of an undisturbed terrain.

There were four of the mounds. All located about a quarter of a mile away from headquarters. The opening Red was looking through was facing the front of the main house. His was a commanding view of the ground that lay before him.

Sandy had stepped-off six hundred feet, and marked the holes two hundred feet apart. He was in the southernmost hole, Tommy was next, then Red, and Pike was at the north end.

This was the Indians' style of fighting an enemy. To let the enemy ride unsuspectingly by, then rise out of the dirt and kill him. And the people in the buildings had been advised to get behind something when the shooting started.

Red thought of the past night. A Tuesday's, October the twenty-ninth, 1872. A half-moon was lighting the land . . . and getting larger. In a few more days a full-moon would be over Kansas. And the Wallace hired gunslingers would have to strike long before then. As each passing night nudged the successful ending of a fight in the Leaning-S's favor.

Red lay in his bedroll. As he did last night . . . belly-down. And watched as the lamps in the main house and bunkhouse were put out. Then the place was quiet. There were no night critters making noise . . . because of the coldness. But off in the distance, the yipping of several coyotes could be heard. And this was of no help to the waiting punchers. Coyotes' will talk to one another, and bark at an intruder. The varmints come close to headquarters at night, and move among the trees along the creek as ghostly shadows.

It was Thursday morning. Just before dawn, when he saw the glow from a lamp in the kitchen. And Red crawled out of the hole with rifle in hand. He arrived in front of the bunkhouse with his three companions.

"Let's give Ma a chance to get the coffee boiling," Red said, "and then surround her table! I am hungry!"

To an observer, the day started as all days do on the spread. The hands and Johansens ate breakfast, and went back to work. With the crew saddling mounts and riding-out. The Johansens resuming work on the barn.

And when this day ended . . . the work stopped. This was just before darkness fell upon the land. Then it was the hour before the moon would appear. The darkest hour of the evening. With a slight cooling wind blowing-in from the northwest.

Red, Tommy, Pike and Sandy headed back to their holes in the ground. And they separated at the creek.

The young foreman backed into his hiding place, and lay on top of the bedroll. His fully loaded Winchester was to his right, and a spare Colt .44-40 was at his left shoulder.

Red listened to the sound of voices coming from the area of the barn. They soon stopped and the lamps were put out again. He was watching the shadows among the trees become smaller, as the moon rose higher in the sky. Then the ground under him began moving.

A distant rumble sounded like thunder. The noise swelled and the ground shook. With Red's heavy body bouncing. Then Leaning-S cattle were spilling over the mound of dirt he was under. The leaders of the stampede were headed straight for the creek and headquarters.

Air heavy with dust boiled into the hole. It had Red covering his mouth and nose with a bandanna, and placing his hat over the back of his head. Then the stampede had passed. The ground stopped shaking, and there was only the sound of cattle moving about in the partially completed barn.

Red raised his head, and saw that dust restricted his vision. Several seconds passed before he tried to see again. The dust was still there. More time went by. With the wind slowly pushing the high cloud of dust to the southeast. Then it moved away from Red's hiding place like a dense fog. And two riders walked their mounts past the mound of dirt. They were following the dust cloud.

"How come old man Wallace doesn't want his son to know about this raid?" Red heard one of them say.

"It's that bitch Brad's married to! She informed Brad that she'd leave him . . . if this redheaded Tubar Lane was hurt!"

"And we're to kill him?"

"Him . . . and everyone on the place!"

"Hell, this will be easy! I rode with Bill Quantrill, and we used this same setup! A stampede, some shooting, and the women and whiskey were ours! We treed many a . . . ."

They rode out of hearing. And Red pushed the barrel of the Winchester out of the hole. Placed the stock against his right shoulder, pulled the hammer back, and waited. He counted ten riders, before Sandy's first shot was heard.

Red pulled the trigger. The big rifle kicked back, and the rider he was aiming at was swept out of the saddle. Then he shot Quantrill's man. His left boot hung in the stirrup and the horse spooked. The frightened animal started running and was kicking at its rider's head at every jump. And there wasn't a man still on a horse.

"COME ON!" Sandy yelled. "LET'S SEE IF ANY OF THEM ARE ALIVE! AND BE DAMN CAREFUL!"

Red crawled out, taking his rifle and spare Colt with him. He transferred the Winchester to his left hand. Then cat-footed up to the first man he shot.

"Is he dead?" Sandy asked.

"And in hell! I heard my second renegade say he rode with William Clarke Quantrill! A horse was dragging him in that direction!" Red pointed to the north.

"The Army will most likely give you a medal . . . if we take his body in!"

Red shook his head. "Nope . . . I don't want any of his old partners hearing about this!"

Sandy laughed, as Tommy joined them. "Bill Compton trained you real good!"

"Are any of yours among the living?" Red asked Tommy.

"Hell no! I can shoot as good as you can, Yank!"

"Then let's see how Pike did!"

Tommy and Sandy followed their young boss toward Pike's hole in the ground. And found him with a prisoner.

"Where are the rest of them?" Sandy asked.

"I tallied two," Pike answered, "and they're over there!" He pointed in the direction of the creek. "But I only grazed this son of a bitch's shoulder! It was enough to knock him out of the saddle! Then I was on him!"

Red stared at the man. Who was sitting on the ground. "How many were in your gang?" Red didn't get an answer. "I counted ten, Sandy!"

"We have eight dead . . . plus the bastard the horse dragged off!" Sandy said. "And this one makes ten! What do you want done with him?"

"Find a horse with a lariat tied to the saddle!" Red answered.

Pike and Tommy escorted the silent gunman to the row of trees on their side of the creek. Then stopped under the highest tree. And Sandy appeared leading a horse.

He cut a short piece off of a lariat, and pitched it to Pike. Then formed a hanging-noose, while the gunslinger's hands were being tied behind him.

Sandy placed the noose around the man's neck . . . with the slip-knot at his right ear. And they bodily put the gunman in the saddle. Then the ex-Army scout threw the other end of the lariat over a high limb. He wound the lariat around the tree-trunk several times, and tied it.

Red used his skinning knife to cut a long switch off of the same tree. With the captured renegade watching him. And Red walked to the rear end of the horse. Then stopped, and spoke to him. "Do you have anything to say?"

"Go to hell!"

Red brought the switch down hard across the horse's rump.

* * * *

The grim-faced foreman left the gunman swinging, and led his crew of three determined cowhands across the creek and toward the bunkhouse. James, Mister Johansen and his sons, came to meet them.

"Go tell Ma none of us were injured, James!" Red instructed the boy. "And that we bagged all ten of Russell Wallace's gunhands!"

"We could not see to shoot!" Ingrid's father said, as James left them. "Too much dust and cattle!"

Red ran his eyes over the older man. He was wearing Pippen's gunbelt, and holding his Winchester. "There are ten dead men over there! One is hanging from the limb of a tree, eight are on the ground, and one was dragged-off by his horse! He'll have to be found, along with their mounts!"

Mister Johansen nodded his head. "We will bury the bastards, Red! Just show us where to do it!"

"I'd appreciate that!" Red replied, and turned to Sandy. "I want Ma and Ingrid to leave for town right away! You, Pike and Tommy are to take them in!"

"We'll saddle the horses," Sandy said, "and be ready to ride when they are!"

"Is it safe to ride my Black?" Mister Johansen asked Red.

The Leaning-S foreman nodded his head. "You can take your horse any damn place you want to now!"

"Then I'm going too!" And Mister Johansen turned to Rolv. "You bury the dead!"

Red watched Mister Johansen until he was almost to the corral. Then headed in the opposite direction . . . toward the kitchen. And found his Ma, Missus Johansen, James and Ingrid, seated at the table. The blonde-headed woman rose to her feet and came to meet him. Red reached for Ingrid's hands, while speaking to his Ma.

"Put some riding clothes on! You and Ingrid are leaving for town!" Then Red looked into Ingrid's blue eyes. "I'm in love with you, beautiful woman! Will you marry me?"

"I do . . . I do!"

"That's not the right answer!"

Ingrid laughed, as Starlet left the kitchen. "Yes . . . it is! I'm practicing!"

"Mother Johansen . . . do you object to me marrying your daughter?"

"No, son! But you must ask Ingrid's father for her hand! His ways are old!"

"Red," Starlet said from her bedroom, "what is so urgent about us leaving for town now?"

"I want you to see Elsa as soon as you get there! Tell her that I'll ride in at three o'clock! And if Brad is still in Dodge City . . . I'm going to kill him!"

* * * *

Starlet, Ingrid, Pike, Tommy and Sandy, were waiting in front of the Dodge House when Red arrived. It was straight-up three o'clock. Sandy tied the Bay to the hitching-rail. And watched his young partner climb out of the saddle.

"Brad's not here! He and Elsa left on the noon passenger train!"

Red nodded his head, with a deep feeling of relief. "That's damn good news, Sandy! I didn't want to hurt Elsa!" Then Red continued to Ingrid. "Where's your father?"

"He's at Zimmermann's gun shop . . . looking at revolvers!"

Red laughed. "Let's talk to him now! While he's in a good mood!"

The End